GALLUP
MAJOR TRENDS & EVENTS
The Pulse of Our Nation: 1900 to the Present

Abortion

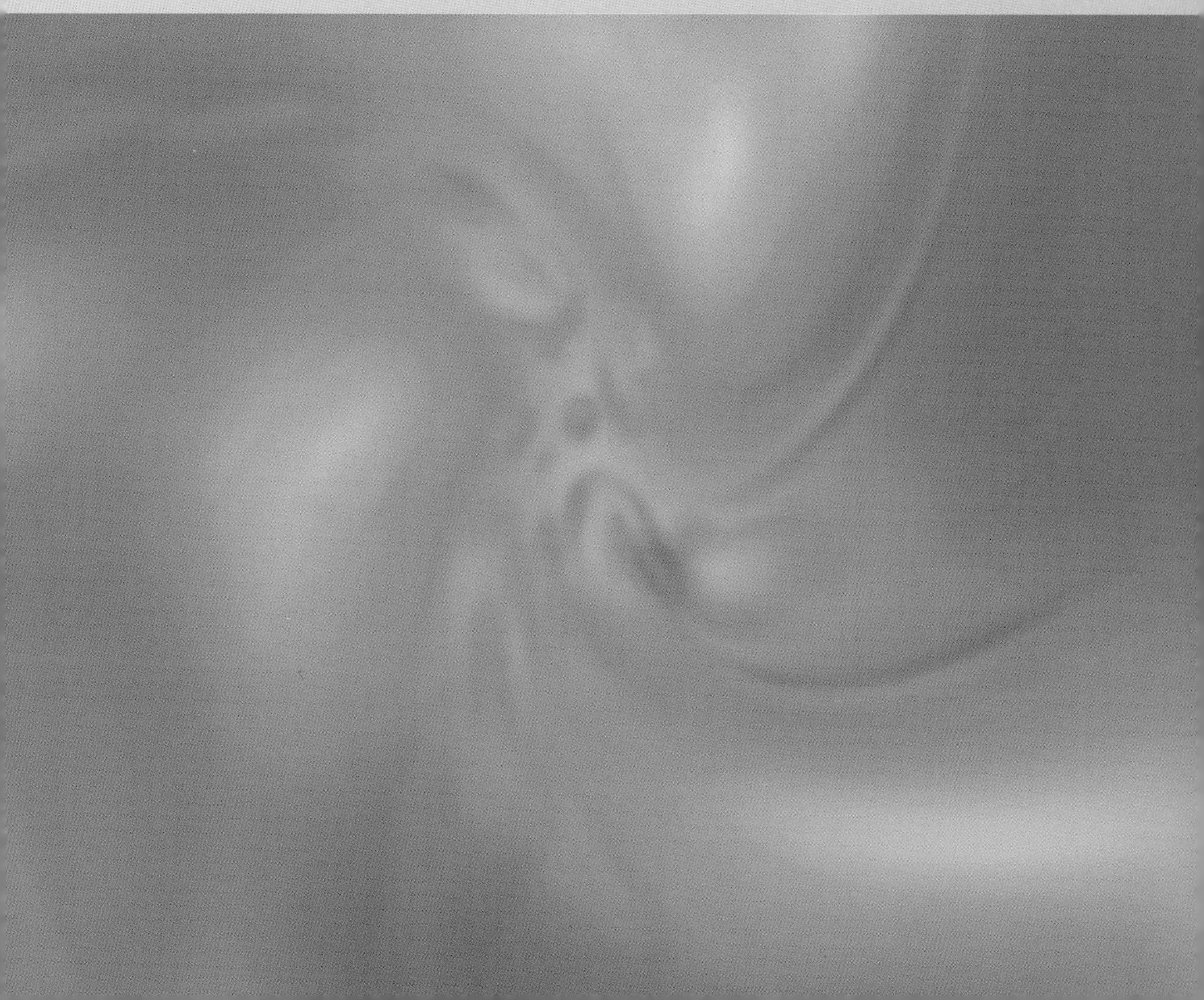

GALLUP
MAJOR TRENDS & EVENTS
The Pulse of Our Nation: 1900 to the Present

Abortion

Drug & Alcohol Abuse

Health Care

Immigration

Marriage & Family Issues

Obesity

Race Relations

Technology

GALLUP
MAJOR TRENDS & EVENTS
The Pulse of Our Nation: 1900 to the Present

Abortion

Hal Marcovitz

Produced by OTTN Publishing, Stockton, New Jersey

Mason Crest Publishers
370 Reed Road
Broomall, PA 19008
www.masoncrest.com

3 5 7 9 8 6 4 2

Library of Congress Cataloging-in-Publication Data

Marcovitz, Hal.
Abortion / Hal Marcovitz.
p. cm. — (Gallup major trends and events)
Includes index.
ISBN-13: 978-1-59084-962-0 (hard cover)
ISBN-10: 1-59084-962-0 (hard cover)
1. Abortion—Juvenile literature. I. Title. II. Series.
HQ767.M374 2006
363.46—dc22

2005016296

TABLE OF CONTENTS

Photo by Eric Olesen

Introduction

By Alec Gallup, Chairman, The Gallup Poll

In ways both obvious and subtle, the United States of today differs significantly from the United States that existed at the turn of the 20th century. In 1900, for example, America had not yet taken its place among the world's most influential nations; today the United States stands by itself as the globe's lone superpower. The 1900 census counted about 76 million Americans, largely drawn from white European peoples such as the English, Irish, and Germans; 100 years later the U.S. population was approaching 300 million, and one in every eight residents was of Hispanic origin. In the first years of the 20th century, American society offered women few opportunities to pursue professional careers, and, in fact, women had not yet gained the right to vote. Though slavery had been abolished, black Americans 100 years ago continued to be treated as second-class citizens, particularly in the South, where the Jim Crow laws that would endure for another half-century kept the races separate and unequal.

The physical texture and the pace of American life, too, were much different 100 years ago—or, for that matter, even 50 years ago. Accelerating technological and scientific progress, a hallmark of modern times, has made possible a host of innovations that Americans today take for granted but that would have been unimaginable three generations ago—from brain scans to microwave ovens to cell phones, laptop computers, and the Internet.

No less important than the material, social, and political changes the United States has witnessed over the past century are the changes in American attitudes and perceptions. For example, the way Americans relate to their government and their fellow citizens, how they view marriage and child-rearing norms, where they set the boundary between society's responsibilities and the individual's rights and freedoms—all are key components of Americans' evolving understanding of their nation and its place in the world.

The books in this series examine important issues that have perennially concerned (and sometimes confounded) Americans since the turn of the 20th century. Each volume draws on an array of sources to provide vivid detail and historical context. But, as suggested by the series title, GALLUP MAJOR TRENDS AND EVENTS: THE PULSE OF OUR NATION, 1900 TO THE PRESENT, these books make particular use of the Gallup Organization's vast archive of polling data.

There is perhaps no better source for tracking and understanding American public opinion than Gallup, a name that has been synonymous with opinion polling for seven decades. Over the years, Gallup has elicited responses from more than 3.5 million people on more than 125,000 questions. In 1936 the organization, then known as the American Institute of Public Opinion, emerged into the spotlight when it correctly predicted that Franklin Roosevelt would be reelected president of the United States. This directly contradicted the well-respected Literary Digest Poll, which had announced that Alfred Landon, governor of Kansas, would not only become president but would win in a landslide. Since then Gallup polls have not simply been a fixture in election polling and analysis; they have also cast light on public opinion regarding a broad variety of social, economic, and cultural issues.

Polling results tend to be most noticed during political campaigns or in the wake of important events; during these times, polling provides snapshots of public opinion. This series, however, is more concerned with long-term attitude trends than with responses to breaking news. Thus data from many years of Gallup polls are used to trace the evolution of American attitudes. How, for example, have Americans historically viewed immigration? Did attitudes toward foreign newcomers shift during the Great Depression, after the 1941 Japanese attack on Pearl Harbor, or after the terrorist attacks of September 11, 2001? Do opinions on immigration vary across different age, gender, and ethnic groups?

Or, taking another particularly divisive issue treated in this series, what did Americans think about abortion during the many decades the procedure was generally illegal? How has public opinion changed since the Supreme Court's landmark 1973 *Roe v. Wade* decision? How many Americans now favor overturning *Roe*?

By understanding where we as a society have been, we can better understand where we are—and, sometimes, where we are going.

1 THE ISSUE THAT DIVIDES AMERICA

Pro-life and pro-choice activists hold up signs while demonstrating outside the U.S. Supreme Court in Washington, D.C. Since the Supreme Court's 1973 *Roe v. Wade* decision, the country has become bitterly divided on the issue of abortion.

Over the course of its history, the United States has faced many contentious social and political issues. In most instances, controversy and conflict have eventually given way to compromise and consensus. Such is not the case with abortion. More than a century ago, the American public began wrestling with the question of whether it was permissible for a woman to terminate a pregnancy. Today the issue continues to inspire as much rancor, divisiveness, and inflexibility as ever.

For nearly three-quarters of the 20th century, abortion was for the most part illegal in the United States. It was criminalized not only out of concern for the life of the unborn—which is the overriding motivation driving anti-abortion activists today—but also because doctors argued that the procedures for surgically terminating a pregnancy were unsafe for women.

Abortion had always been an issue over which the states demanded local control, and state legislatures adopted a smorgasbord of laws regulating the procedure. Most of these laws permitted abortion only in cases of rape or incest or when the life of the mother was endangered by her pregnancy. For everyone else, abortion was illegal.

But that is not to say women didn't seek abortions. For decades, pregnant women—including many teenage girls—got "back alley" abortions, performed by midwives and other abortionists operating outside the law. Infections and deaths were common. In the years leading up to the decriminalization of abortion, it is believed that some 5,000 women died each year from botched abortions.

Ironically, the very type of abortionists the doctors hoped to drive out of business by making abortion illegal simply moved their shady practices underground.

In the 1960s, concern for women's health, along with a budding women's rights movement, led to growing calls for the legalization of abortion on demand. This would permit doctors to perform the procedure under safe conditions. In 1973 the U.S. Supreme Court handed down its landmark *Roe v. Wade* decision, making abortion legal for any woman (and for any reason) before the third trimester of pregnancy. Since then, pregnancies have been terminated by the millions.

Adult Views on Abortion, 1975

"Do you think abortions should be legal under any circumstances, only under certain circumstances, or illegal in all circumstances?"

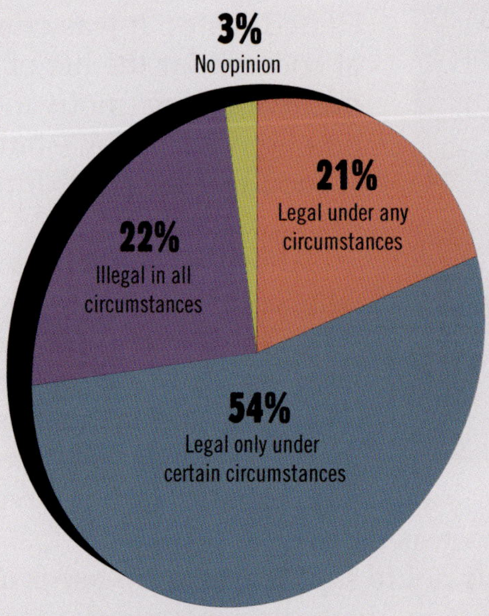

Poll taken April 1975; 1,535 total respondents
Source: The Gallup Organization

BIRTH OF THE ANTI-ABORTION MOVEMENT

The Supreme Court's decision in *Roe v. Wade* gave birth to the nation's anti-abortion movement. Practically overnight, opponents of abortion mobilized and assumed the duty of protecting the rights of the unborn. Although their efforts have fallen short of the ultimate goal of overturning *Roe v. Wade*, anti-abortion advocates have been successful in chipping away at the Court's blanket approval of first- and second-trimester abortions. For example, many states now have parental consent laws that require teenage girls to receive their parents' permission before undergoing an abortion. Many states also impose mandatory waiting periods. A federal law passed in 2003 banned a controversial technique used to terminate late-stage pregnancies (though court challenges to the prohibition quickly arose). And three of the five presidents elected since the *Roe v. Wade* decision pledged their support to abortion opponents.

By 2005, with a socially conservative president (George W. Bush) in the White House and a conservative Republican majority in the U.S. Senate, many abortion rights advocates warned that the complete reversal of *Roe v. Wade* might be only a matter of time. That's because presidents nominate, and the Senate confirms, members of the federal judiciary—including Supreme Court justices—and conservative judicial nominees might be expected to take a dim view of legalized abortion. In particular, abortion rights advocates worried about the closely divided Supreme Court. With the retirement of Associate Justice Sandra Day O'Connor and the death of Chief Justice William Rehnquist, it appeared that President Bush might have the opportunity to create a solid conservative majority on the Court for years to come—and this majority might welcome the chance to revisit *Roe*. Yet, as many legal observers pointed out, presidents have often been surprised and confounded at the way their nominees voted once on the Supreme Court. It was, for example, a nominee of President Richard M. Nixon—a relatively conservative Republican—who wrote the Court's *Roe v. Wade* decision.

WHERE THE PUBLIC STANDS

The Gallup Organization, a national polling institute, has gauged public opinion on abortion since before the *Roe v. Wade* decision. It has found notable consistency on the issue. Essentially, a little less than one in four Americans believes that abortion should be legal under any circumstances, while a little less than one in five believes that it should be illegal under any circumstances.

So who is in the middle? According to Gallup, about 54 percent of Americans feel abortion should be legal only under some circumstances, but those circumstances never seem to be clearly defined. For example, the majority of Americans seem willing to defend a woman's right to obtain an abortion, but they find late-term abortions unseemly and unnecessary. They also believe that the Supreme Court should let *Roe v. Wade* stand, but they have told pollsters that they favor more restrictions on abortion. Said a 2004 Gallup analysis, "While Americans generally oppose an unrestricted right to an abortion, several polls have shown a consistent majority opposition to overturning the *Roe v. Wade* decision."

In the communities of people who support or oppose abortion rights, the terms *pro-choice* and *pro-life* are common. Both sides complain about how their opponents have elected to designate themselves. People who regard themselves as pro-choice insist that they support a woman's right to choose. People who are pro-life believe there is only one choice to be made, and that is to choose the life of the baby. Some pro-life people say that pro-choice people *favor* abortion. Pro-choice people disagree, insisting that they support abstinence, contraception, and adoption, but that women should still have the freedom to terminate their pregnancies through abortion. Many pro-choice activists think that calling the other side pro-life somehow suggests that people who support abortion rights do not believe a baby's life is important.

Despite the fight over rhetoric, the terms have remained a part of the American vocabulary. According to a 2005 Gallup poll, 48 percent of Americans regard themselves as pro-choice, while 45 percent call themselves pro-life.

The debate, never settled in the 20th century, remains unsettled in the 21st. And if the past is any guide, the issue of abortion will continue to divide Americans for generations to come.

Current Views on Abortion

"With respect to the abortion issue, would you consider yourself to be pro-choice or pro-life?"

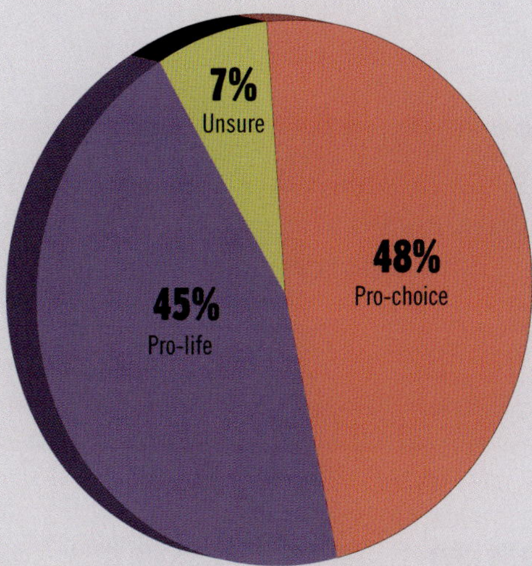

Poll taken May 2005; 1,005 total respondents
Source: The Gallup Organization

2 THE CRIME OF ABORTION

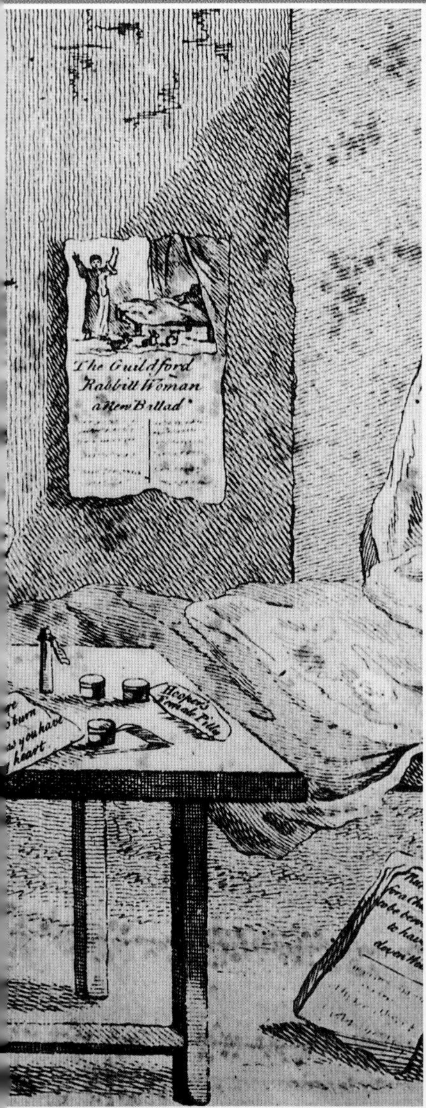

"The Pills have sav'd my Child's Honour," a woman tells an abortionist in this 18th-century woodcut cartoon. Until the second half of the 19th century, abortion was generally legal in the United States if performed before quickening.

By the early 1900s, abortion was for the most part illegal throughout the United States. There were exceptions—in many states the procedure could be legally performed in cases of rape or incest or when it was believed the life of the mother was placed in jeopardy by the pregnancy. For everyone else, abortion was illegal. Married and single women, including young girls, were denied abortions under law.

Until this era, though, abortion was widely available in America. Indeed, dating back to colonial times any woman or teenage girl could get an abortion as long as she knew an abortionist and had the money to pay for the procedure. Most state laws permitted abortions before "quickening"—the first time movement by the fetus is felt. (The onset of quickening varies but usually falls around 16 to 20 weeks into the pregnancy.) Today, most anti-abortion activists argue that life begins at conception and that even an embryo at its earliest stages has the right to grow into a baby. But as late as the first half of the 19th century, abortion before the onset of quickening was generally legal.

The criminalization of abortion came about largely through the efforts of the American Medical Association (AMA), which waged a "physicians' crusade" against the procedure in the years following the Civil War. At that time, only a handful of states outlawed abortion. The anti-abortion movement within the AMA was led by Boston physician Horatio Robinson Storer. The Harvard University–educated doctor had a variety of reasons for opposing abortion, some principled and others hopelessly narrow-minded by today's standards. On the one hand,

Storer was a tireless advocate for improving women's health care, and he recognized the serious dangers posed by abortion procedures. He also suggested that life might begin at conception, making abortion morally wrong. On the other hand, Storer was vehemently opposed to the idea of women becoming doctors, and as he believed that female physicians would naturally fill the niche of abortion providers, banning abortion was a way to discourage women from making inroads into the medical profession. Furthermore, Storer wanted to preserve the white, Protestant character of the nation at a time when the United States was expanding westward and accepting new, sparsely inhabited territories such as Colorado, North Dakota, South Dakota, Montana, and Wyoming into the Union. Permitting abortion, he argued, would lower birthrates among native-born, white, Protestant Americans and thereby enable what in his view were less desirable groups—immigrants, blacks, Chinese, Indians, Catholics, Jews—to settle the new territories. "Shall [these states] be filled by our own children or by those of aliens?" he asked in 1868. "This is a question our women must answer; upon their loins depends the future destiny of the nation."

Storer was joined in his condemnation of abortion by many of the feminists of the era, albeit for different reasons. These early feminists were the predecessors of the abortion rights activists of today, but they nevertheless found abortion abhorrent. Women's suffrage activist Susan B. Anthony called abortion "child murder" and said, "No matter what the motive, love of ease, or a desire to save from suffering the unborn innocent, the woman is awfully guilty who commits the deed. It will burden her conscience in life, it will burden her soul in death." The anarchist Emma Goldman, a staunch defender of birth control, found no reason to support abortion. She suggested that poor, working-class women were driven to terminating their pregnancies by the social conditions of the day. "The custom of

Susan B. Anthony (left) and Emma Goldman took different approaches to gaining greater rights for women in American society. In their opposition to abortion, however, the two early feminists were in agreement.

procuring abortions has reached such appalling proportions in America," she said, "as to be beyond belief. . . . So great is the misery of the working classes that seventeen abortions are committed in every one hundred pregnancies."

A RISKY PROCEDURE

But working-class women were by no means the only ones who sought abortions, and rich or poor, all faced the possibility of serious harm. Even when performed by a trained medical professional, abortion posed substantial risks to the pregnant woman's health. The risks were magnified when the abortionist was a midwife or simply a person who advertised his or her services in the local newspaper alongside the offers for palm readings and health elixirs.

Drinking excessive amounts of alcohol, drinking whiskey mixed with gunpowder, and even swallowing turpentine were a few of the ways pregnant women in earlier times sought to induce miscarriage.

Many women desperate to end an unwanted pregnancy turned first to nonsurgical options. Drug and herbal treatments included quinine, savin, pennyroyal, tansy, ergot, and seneca snakeroot. Unfortunately, the dosages required to produce a miscarriage could, in many instances, be toxic to the woman. Eschewing herbal treatments, some women drank whiskey mixed with gunpowder or even the starch they used on their husbands' shirts. Others swallowed turpentine (which, because it caused vomiting, was thought to induce miscarriage). Still others tried an essentially harmless folk remedy such as drinking a glass of water in which a rusty nail had been soaked. Other home remedies included bathing in steaming water, jumping down steps, and lifting heavy weights. Some women even sought someone to punch them in the abdomen.

If these measures failed, many women faced the prospect of visiting an abortionist. At best the operation was unpleasant. The abortionist might insert a rubber tube or ball of gauze into the cervix, hoping to irritate the muscles and cause contractions. If that didn't work, the abortionist might force open the cervix with metal tongs, then insert a long, spoon-like instrument known as a curette into the womb to scrape the placenta out of the uterus. That method was exceedingly painful. A doctor might employ a crude anesthesia, such as ether or chloroform, to ease the pain; a midwife might offer nothing stronger than whiskey.

Serious complications arose frequently from abortion procedures. Infections were common, and antibacterial drugs to treat them did not yet exist. Internal bleeding also caused many deaths.

Medical considerations were a large part of the reason for the successes of the "physicians' crusade" to stamp out abortion in the United States. By the end of the 19th century, Dr. Storer and the AMA and their allies had convinced every state legislature to outlaw the procedure except in cases of rape or incest or when the mother's health was in danger. (Some states weren't even that lenient; the Texas abortion law, on the books since 1857, did not regard rape as a legitimate reason for aborting a fetus.)

"FROM EVERY WALK OF LIFE"

Just because laws prohibited abortion doesn't mean the practice stopped, however. Women who didn't want to have babies were still getting pregnant. Many were unmarried and did not want to live with the stigma of being an unwed mother. It was not unusual, though, for married couples to seek abortions. In many cases, the decision was based on financial considerations—families felt they could not afford more children. Also, women worried about their health. Childbirth was still a dangerous experience, and many women feared the consequences of a difficult delivery.

By the turn of the 20th century, it was estimated that some 2 million American women obtained abortions each year, even though the procedure had been outlawed. In 1911 Dr. J. Henry Barbat, a prominent California physician, said, "Those who apply for abortions are from every walk of life, from the factory girl to the millionaire's daughter; from the laborer's wife to that of the banker, no class, no sect seems to be above . . . the destruction of the fetus."

Anti-abortion crusaders were forced to admit that the public had not united behind their efforts. And even though the AMA had spearheaded the crusade against abortion, it was clear that divisions over the issue also existed within the medical profession. In fact, many prominent members of the AMA continued to perform abortions themselves. In 1904 Nebraska physician Inez Philbrook said, "The chief responsibility for the prevalence of criminal abortion rests upon the medical profession. In every community, members of the profession live by its induction." Four years later, Dr. Rudolph Holmes, chairman of a Chicago Medical Society committee given the job of exposing abortion-practicing doctors, finally conceded, "I have come to the conclusion that the public does not want, the profession does not want, the women in particular do not want, any aggressive campaign against the crime of abortion."

The continued practice of abortion was an open secret in American society. "The United States," an anonymous physician wrote in a medical journal in 1920, "tolerates abortion done within the bounds of discreet secrecy." In the late 1920s, a study of 10,000 women who attended Margaret Sanger's birth control clinics indicated that 20 percent of them had ended their pregnancies through abortion. A 1931 study at a New York City birth control clinic found that 35 percent of the center's 1,000 clients admitted to having obtained an abortion.

While clients of birth control clinics weren't necessarily representative of the population at large—and thus it would be impossible to extrapolate from these statistics how many abortions were being performed throughout the United States—various studies indicated that abortion rates overall rose during the 1930s. Economic conditions probably played a major role in this trend. The stock market crash of 1929 ushered in the Great Depression, a time when millions of Americans suddenly found themselves out of work. For many women, whether they were single or married, the cost of raising children now seemed prohibitive. One study found that in New Orleans, illegal abortions increased by 166 percent from 1930 to 1931. Later, associates of sex researcher Alfred C. Kinsey wrote, "The depression of the 1930's resulted in a

Farmers wait in line to receive federal relief during the Great Depression. The hard economic times of the 1930s, various studies indicate, were accompanied by higher rates of abortion in the United States.

larger proportion of pregnancies that were artificially aborted."

Evidence indicates that high rates of abortion continued through World War II. The United States entered that conflict in late 1941; the war ended in 1945.

During the 1930s and 1940s, the state of affairs with regard to abortion recalled aspects of the Prohibition period (1920–33), during which the manufacture, transport, and sale of alcohol were illegal. As with the alcohol ban, the abortion laws were broken by a large number of people. Nor was there a wide public call for the total elimination of abortion. Still, the authorities in many jurisdictions vigorously enforced the laws. Many police departments established squads specifically to raid abortion clinics—much as they had crashed through the doors of bootlegging operations during the years of Prohibition. Patients as well as doctors were arrested in the abortion clinic raids. Meanwhile, state legislatures moved to strengthen their anti-abortion laws. In 1942, for example, the governor of New York signed a law that prohibited doctors from providing their patients with referrals to abortionists. Later, a prosecutor in an Illinois case told the *Chicago Daily News*, "A large percentage of the medical profession is winking at the violation of abortion laws. . . . [D]octors can be charged as accessories to criminal violations if they steer such patients."

The renewed zeal for enforcing anti-abortion laws occurred during a time not simply when the abortion rate continued to climb but also when the maternal mortality rate attributed to abortion began to drop. By now, midwives had largely been driven out of the abortion business. Physicians were now specializing in obstetrics. The development of sulfa drugs and then penicillin meant fewer infections. By the late 1940s it was statistically safer for a woman to have a first-trimester abortion than to deliver a baby.

CHANGING ATTITUDES

During the 1950s, attitudes toward abortion began to shift among professional organizations and even law enforcement agencies. The American Medical Association softened its century-old stance against abortion, calling for a decriminalization of the procedure. In 1959 the American Law Institute—a national organization composed of prominent judges, lawyers, and law professors—urged state legislatures to make abortion legal. Some police departments quietly disbanded their abortion clinic squads.

In 1958 associates of Alfred Kinsey, who had died two years before, published the results of an extensive study titled *Pregnancy, Birth and Abortion*. The researchers at Kinsey's Indiana University Institute of Sex Research wrote:

> We find that defense lawyers know that their best way to win an abortion case is to secure a jury rather than a court trial. Police and other officials often allow known

> abortionists to practice since it is felt that there is a need for their services. . . . In our own sample we find that the great percentage of women who had an illegal abortion stated that it had been the best solution to their immediate problem. This widespread difference between our overt culture as expressed in our laws and public pronouncements and our covert culture as expressed in what people actually do and secretly think is as true with abortion as with most types of sexual behavior.

The Indiana University researchers claimed to have interviewed one abortionist who performed no less

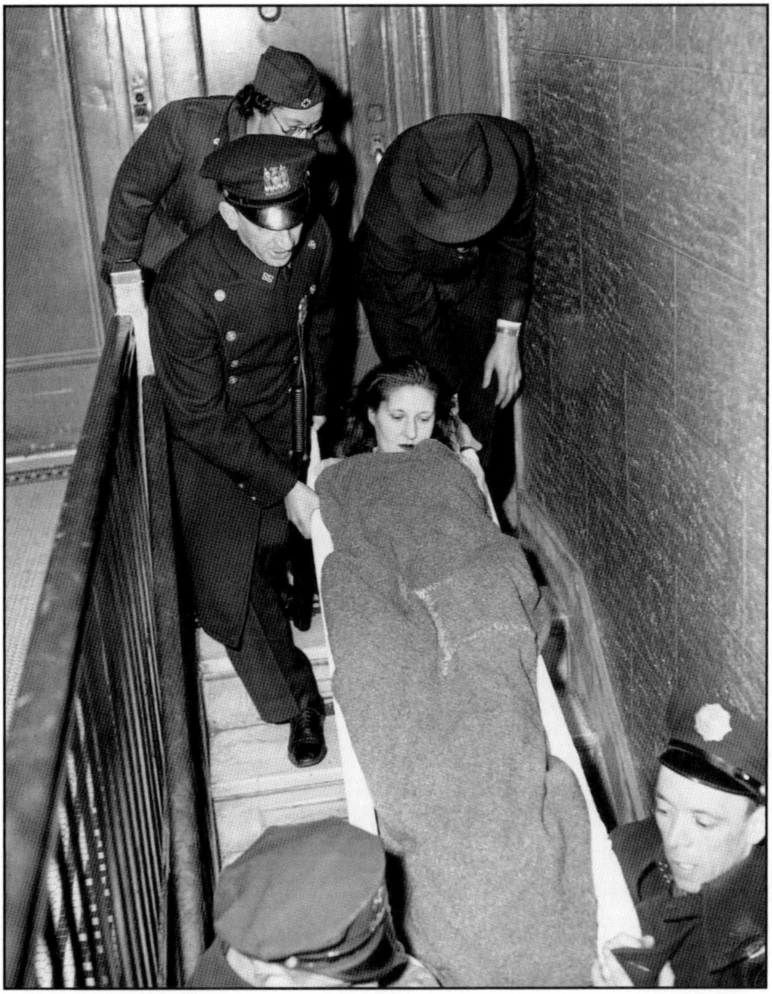

Although attitudes toward abortion began to change during the 1950s, police continued to enforce the laws banning abortion. Here, at the conclusion of a police raid, officers carry a woman out of an apartment where a doctor was performing an illegal abortion.

than 30,000 procedures—all of them illegal. What's more, the researchers confirmed what other studies had been saying for decades: a huge number of women were having their pregnancies terminated. After conducting interviews with more than 5,000 women, the Indiana University researchers found that 18 percent of the unmarried respondents under the age of 36 had undergone an abortion, while another 8 percent over the age of 36 had gone through the procedure. Of the married women who participated in the study, the researchers found that between one-fifth and one-quarter of the respondents received abortions.

The researchers found that although some women were troubled by their decision to have an abortion, the psychological scars were generally not long lasting, and subsequent medical complications were few. Said the Kinsey institute's researchers:

> Abortion is considered murder in some systems of law and philosophy, yet less than 10 per cent of the females in the present sample reported psychological upset over their induced abortions. In most cases this was given in general terms . . . they were emotionally upset or, in a smaller number of cases, they were depressed or had guilty feelings. A few said they were nervous for some time after the abortion. One regretted a subsequent sterility, one almost committed suicide, one reported that it affected her subsequent sexual relations adversely, another that she was "ruined mentally." Hence although in the great majority of cases there appears to be little psychological trauma, a considerable amount of unfavorable reaction does show up in a few cases. As might be expected, women married at the time of abortion showed less of the psychological after-effects than the single females.

The institute's statistics showed that many women wanted abortions and were finding ways to get them. The medical community had softened its position on abortion. Legal experts urged its decriminalization. And yet, the state legislatures responded slowly. Most states modestly expanded the circumstances under which abortions could be obtained. But with few exceptions, abortions were available only to rape and incest victims and women whose lives were placed in danger by their pregnancies. Many states, including Texas, refused to liberalize their abortion laws at all.

In Texas, abortion had been largely banned for more than a century; even rape was not regarded as a valid reason to terminate a pregnancy. But in 1969 a Texas woman named Norma McCorvey found herself pregnant and sought an abortion. She was refused. Under the name of Jane Roe, McCorvey filed a lawsuit against the Texas law, contending it violated her constitutional right to privacy. The case would become known as *Roe v. Wade,* and it would forever change the abortion laws of the United States and force the issue into the forefront of public consciousness and debate.

3

LANDMARK DECISION

To thousands of preschool children in Phoenix, Arizona, Sherri Finkbine was "Miss Sherri," the lighthearted host of *Romper Room*, a daytime TV show that helped children learn how to count, keep time to music by clapping drumsticks together, and follow good manners by heeding the lessons taught by "Mr. Do Bee" and "Mr. Don't Bee." At the end of each show, Miss Sherri would gaze into the "Magic Mirror" and say good-bye to all the children who joined her for the 30-minute broadcast.

At the time she hosted *Romper Room*, Sherri Finkbine was raising her own family. She and her husband, Robert, had four children, and in 1962 Sherri became pregnant with the couple's fifth child.

To help her sleep at night, Sherri took the tranquilizer thalidomide. She would soon learn that thalidomide caused birth defects in babies whose mothers took the drug during pregnancy. The defects were likely to be quite severe—a study in West Germany reported that thalidomide caused babies to be born without arms and legs. Although the U.S. Food and Drug

American television host Sherri Finkbine, accompanied by her husband, Robert, arrives in Sweden in August 1962. Though pregnant with a child with serious birth defects, Finkbine was not permitted to have an abortion in the United States, so she traveled to Sweden to undergo the procedure.

Administration quickly withdrew the drug from distribution, it was too late for Sherri Finkbine.

Fearing their child would be born deformed, the Finkbines asked their doctor to approve an abortion at a Phoenix hospital. At the time, Arizona law permitted abortion only if the mother's life was in danger. To protect themselves against charges of violating such laws, hospitals typically established review boards to assess each case and ensure that the reason for the abortion conformed to the legal code.

In the Finkbines' case, the reason for the abortion did not conform to Arizona law because Sherri's life was not in danger. Still, the Finkbines' doctor approved the procedure and felt confident that the board would permit the abortion. It is likely that the hospital's review board would have quietly approved the abortion, but Sherri—who wanted to warn other pregnant women who had taken thalidomide—told her story to a newspaper reporter. Her name was withheld from the story, but a storm of publicity ensued. In the climate of increased scrutiny, the hospital's review board declined to approve an abortion for Sherri Finkbine.

Sherri Finkbine did receive an abortion, however. The Finkbines flew to Sweden, where abortion had been legal since 1938. There the couple learned that their baby would have been born deformed.

Shortly after the Finkbines arrived home, the Gallup Organization asked this question: "As you may have heard or read, an Arizona woman recently had a legal abortion in Sweden after having taken the drug thalidomide, which has been linked to birth defects. Do you think this woman did the right thing or the wrong thing in having this abortion operation?"

It was the first time Gallup had polled the nation on the abortion question. More than 3,000 people were asked the question. A total of 52 percent of the respondents said they thought the Finkbines were justified in seeking the abortion, while 32 percent said it was wrong for Sherri Finkbine to terminate her pregnancy.

Other questions from the same survey showed that the level of public support for legal abortion was contingent on the reasons an abortion might be performed. By an overwhelming margin (77 percent to 16 percent), respondents said abortion should be legal in cases when the mother's health might be endangered by the pregnancy. But these numbers were reversed when respondents were asked whether abortion should be legal if the family didn't have enough money to support another child: 74 percent said no, while only 15 percent said yes. In cases when the child might be born deformed, a

Opinions About Sherri Finkbine's 1962 Abortion

"As you may have heard or read, an Arizona woman recently had a legal abortion in Sweden after having taken the drug thalidomide, which has been linked to birth defects. Do you think this woman did the right thing or the wrong thing in having this abortion operation?"

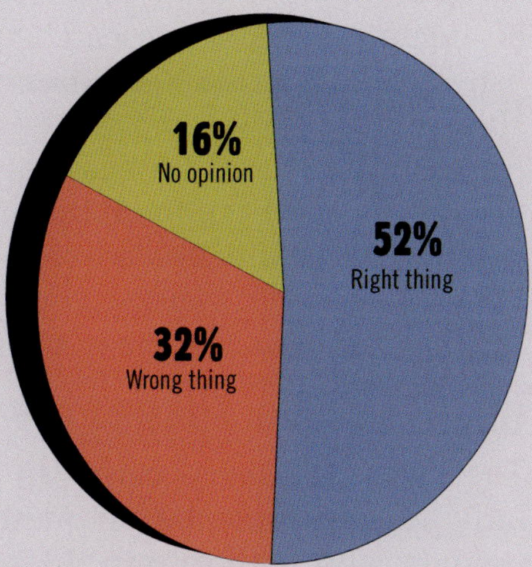

Poll taken August 1962; 3,350 total respondents
Source: The Gallup Organization

majority (55 percent) thought abortion should be a legal option; about 3 in 10 disagreed. Clearly, there was no consensus that the law should restrict access to abortion only to cases of rape, incest, or jeopardy to the mother's life—or that abortion should be legal under any circumstances.

SEXUAL REVOLUTION

Meanwhile, the 1960s were turning out to be an era of great social change in the United States. Women demanded rights they claimed had long been denied to them. In 1963 author Betty Friedan published *The Feminine Mystique*, which told women that there was more to life than being a housewife. The book set the tone for the era of feminism that was soon to begin. Over the next few years, feminist groups would begin lobbying for laws to provide equal employment opportunities for women, including equal pay in the workplace. The demand for "reproductive rights" would soon be added to the feminist agenda as well.

By now, a sexual revolution had also begun. Before his death in 1956, sex researcher Alfred C. Kinsey published two important studies, *Sexual Behavior in the Human Male* (1948) and *Sexual Behavior in the Human Female* (1952). Each showed that sex among single people was far more common than had been believed, and that homosexuality and adultery were widespread. The men's magazine *Playboy* commenced publication in 1953, advising its readers of the pleasures of casual sex.

QUESTIONING AUTHORITY

The 1960s was also a period in which people, particularly young people, began questioning the role of government and authority in their lives. In 1964 the Free Speech Movement was born on the campus of the University of California at Berkeley. Through a series of protests and public demonstrations, students won the right to organize political activity on campus without first receiving the approval of college administrators. Later, students began vehemently opposing American involvement in the Vietnam War; many denied the legitimacy of the government's authority to draft them to fight in that conflict. Meanwhile, in the South, blacks fought hard to win civil rights—and white-dominated state governments resisted them at every turn.

Against this backdrop of social activism and suspicion of the government's motives, issues surrounding abortion increasingly started finding their way into the public consciousness. In 1961 Estelle Griswold, the executive director of the Planned Parenthood League of Connecticut, and Dr. C. Lee Buxton, the chairman of the Yale Medical School department of obstetrics and gynecology, established four Planned Parenthood birth control clinics in Connecticut. Griswold and Buxton were promptly arrested under an 1879 Connecticut law prohibiting the sale of contraceptives, even to married

Estelle Griswold (left) and a supporter flash a victory sign while reading a newspaper article about the Supreme Court decision striking down Connecticut's birth-control law as unconstitutional.

couples. They were convicted on the charge of enhancing the sale of contraceptives by instructing married couples how to use them. Griswold and Buxton appealed, and the case made its way to the U.S. Supreme Court, which overturned the convictions in its 1965 *Griswold v. Connecticut* decision. Justice Potter Stewart said that Connecticut had left an "uncommonly silly law" remaining on its books. What made the Griswold case so important in the abortion question, though, was the Supreme Court's reason for tossing out the law. The Court found that Connecticut's anti-contraceptive law represented an unconstitutional infringement on the right to privacy. In eight years, that finding by the Court would become a pivotal point in the overall question of whether states could legally restrict women's access to abortion.

Gallup polls taken as the Griswold case proceeded through the courts found that the public overwhelmingly supported the distribution of information on birth control. In 1961, shortly before Griswold and Buxton were arrested, 75 percent of the respondents in a Gallup poll said they thought it should be legal to supply birth control information to the public. Just 15 percent said it should be illegal, while 10 percent of the respondents had no opinion. In late 1964, just before the Supreme Court ruled in the Griswold case, the proportion of respondents who favored decriminalizing the distribution of birth control information had grown to 81 percent, with just 11 percent opposed and about 8 percent with no opinion. Clearly, Americans didn't think the government had any business making laws that restricted their access to information about birth control.

A year later, the Gallup Organization published the results of another survey that showed Americans' continued ambivalence toward abortion. Three-quarters (76 percent) of the respondents to the 1965 poll said abortion should be legal in cases when the health of the mother

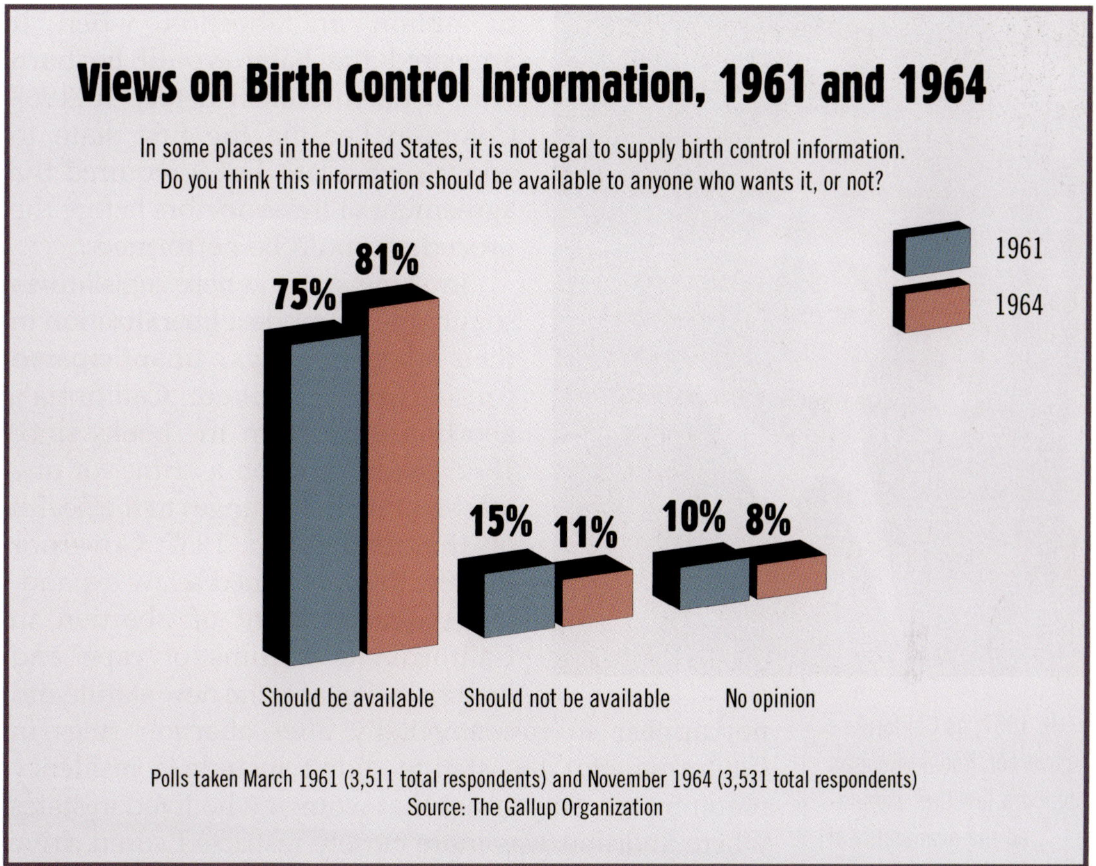

was in danger; a little more than half (53 percent) said abortion should be permitted when the child might be born deformed. However, respondents were overwhelmingly opposed to allowing abortion for reasons of economic hardship: more than 7 in 10 (71 percent) didn't think abortion should be legal just because the family might not have enough money to support another child.

ABORTION LAWS LIBERALIZED

Meanwhile, states were examining their abortion laws. About a third of the states liberalized the laws slightly, widening the definitions that permitted abortion in the case of rape, incest, and health of the mother and adding—in response to the Finkbine case—permission

In 1967, as California's governor, Ronald Reagan signed a law that expanded the availability of abortion. Because the law did not include a residency requirement, women from all over the country could–and did–travel to California to obtain legal abortions.

to obtain an abortion when it appeared the baby would be born with a horrific birth defect. In 1967 Colorado became the first state to adopt such a law, but it required the agreement of three doctors before the procedure could be performed.

In some states whose legislatures sought only a modest liberalization in their abortion laws, unanticipated consequences resulted. California's abortion statute, on the books since 1872, made abortion a crime for any reason other than danger to the health of the mother. In 1967 Governor Ronald Reagan signed a law expanding the availability of abortion in California to victims of rape and incest. On its face, the new statute did not appear to fundamentally alter abortion rules in California. But the statute didn't include a residency requirement. This meant that women who lived in states where abortion was more closely restricted could drive across the border and, claiming to be victims of rape, obtain abortions in California. And that is precisely what happened. According to statistics compiled by Planned Parenthood, 5,018 abortions were performed in California in 1968, the first year the new abortion law was in effect. By 1969 that number had more than tripled. In 1970 more than 65,000 women obtained abortions in California; a year later, the number topped 116,000.

Some states took dramatic steps toward the policy of guaranteeing any woman the right to obtain an abortion as long as her pregnancy had not progressed past the first trimester. In New York, Governor Nelson Rockefeller established a Commission on Abortion Reform to study the issue. In 1968 the panel recommended a liberalization of the abortion laws in order to cut down on illegal abortions, make abortion procedures clean and safe, and give poor women access to abortion.

The results of a November 1969 Gallup poll showed that most Americans were still uncomfortable with the idea that abortion should be legal under all circumstances, though the percentage of respondents willing to accept economic hardship and possible birth defects in the child as legitimate reasons for allowing abortion rose over the numbers recorded in the 1965 and 1962 Gallup polls. Now 23 percent would permit abortion if the family didn't have enough money to support another child, and 62 percent if there was a risk the child would be born deformed. Acceptance of abortion to protect the mother's health remained about the same, at 78 percent. In response to a new question, only 15 percent would allow abortion if the parents simply decided their families were already large enough.

RIPE FOR A COURT CHALLENGE

In 1970 Hawaii became the first state to eliminate criminal penalties for abortion; it was followed by Alaska, Washington, and New York. In New York, Rockefeller signed into law an act repealing the state's 1830 statute outlawing abortion, making the procedure a private matter between a woman and her physician. Also that year, the American Medical Association—the organization that was chiefly responsible for the criminalization of abortion in the 19th century—adopted a resolution permitting doctors to perform abortions for reasons other than the health of the mother or deformity of the child. The decision left it up to the individual doctor to decide whether to perform abortions.

Some states took no action. Texas allowed its restrictive, century-old abortion law to remain on the books. The challenge to that statute would lead to a change in the nation's abortion laws, allowing millions of women to terminate unwanted pregnancies.

In 1969 a 21-year-old waitress named Norma McCorvey learned she was pregnant. McCorvey wanted an abortion, but the Texas state law in effect since 1857 prohibited abortion except in cases when the health of the mother was in danger. Even McCorvey's claim that she had been raped did not qualify her for an abortion under Texas law. (Years later, McCorvey acknowledged publicly that she had not been raped.)

McCorvey's plight came to the attention of Sarah Weddington and Linda Coffee, young activist lawyers who believed the restrictive state law was ripe for a court challenge. In 1970 they filed a class-action lawsuit in Dallas challenging the constitutionality of the Texas abortion law. To protect McCorvey's privacy, the name of the lead plaintiff in the case was "Jane Roe." The suit asked the federal district court to bar the local district attorney, Henry Wade, from enforcing the state's abortion law. The case became known as *Roe v. Wade*.

In 1970, Norma McCorvey sued over Texas's restrictive anti-abortion statute. Eventually, the U.S. Supreme Court would decide her case.

In Dallas the district court ruled that the Texas law was vague and too broad, finding that the statute infringed on a woman's "fundamental right to choose whether to have children." The court ruled that Jane Roe could not be denied an abortion but refused to bar further enforcement of the existing law. Both sides appealed the ruling to the Supreme Court.

It would take three years for the Supreme Court to hand down a decision in *Roe v. Wade*. That was, of course, too late to have an effect on Norma McCorvey's pregnancy. The courts act slowly, to be sure, while pregnancies are over within nine months. As attorneys filed briefs in the case, McCorvey had her baby. She placed the girl up for adoption.

On January 22, 1973, the Supreme Court, by a vote of seven to two, issued its ruling in

Roe v. Wade, finding that all state laws barring or restricting abortions during the first three months of pregnancy violated a woman's fundamental right to privacy. Writing for the majority, Justice Harry Blackmun said the right to privacy—which had been established in the Griswold case—"is broad enough to encompass a woman's decision whether or not to terminate her pregnancy." The decision did not insist, though, that women should have unfettered access to abortion throughout a pregnancy. Instead, Blackmun believed that the state's right (and responsibility) to regulate abortion increased as the pregnancy advanced. He issued a number of guidelines delineating the relative rights of the woman and the state, based on which trimester the pregnancy had reached:

Harry Blackmun wrote the majority opinion in *Roe v. Wade*, the landmark 1973 Supreme Court decision that overturned all state laws prohibiting abortion.

- ✓ During the first three months of pregnancy, the decision to terminate a pregnancy is entirely up to the woman and her doctor. The government has no compelling interest in protecting the woman at this point, Blackmun wrote, because the abortion procedure is as safe as (or even safer than) delivering a baby.
- ✓ During the second three months, a state government may regulate abortion to ensure that the health of the mother is not compromised by the procedure. Blackmun suggested that states would do well to license doctors and abortion clinics. Still, the Court's ruling permitted abortion until the point of fetal viability—generally regarded to be the 24th week. Fetal viability is the point at which the fetus is considered capable of living outside the womb.

✓ During the third trimester—a period that would begin in the 25th week of pregnancy—the fetus is regarded as viable. Therefore, Blackmun wrote, the state has a responsibility to prohibit abortion to protect the interests of the baby, except in cases in which the pregnancy or delivery might endanger the life of the mother.

Blackmun and the other six justices voting in the majority rejected the notion that life begins at conception. Wrote Blackmun, "The word 'person,' as used in the [Constitution], does not include the unborn."

Justices Byron White and William Rehnquist wrote dissenting opinions. White said that "nothing in the language or history of the Constitution" supported the notion that abortion should be available on demand. He urged the Court to leave the issue up to the state legislatures. Rehnquist agreed, pointing out that state legislatures had fashioned their own versions of abortion laws for a century. "The Court's sweeping invalidation of any restrictions on abortion during the first trimester," he wrote, "is impossible to justify. . . . The fact that a majority of the States reflecting, after all, the majority sentiment in those States, have had restrictions on abortions for at least a century is a strong indication, it seems to me, that the asserted right to an abortion is not 'so rooted in the traditions and conscience of our people as to be ranked as fundamental.' "

Nevertheless, in one sweeping order, the Supreme Court tossed out abortion laws in all 50 states. Abortion opponents were shocked beyond belief. For more than a century—since the days when Horatio Storer and the American Medical Association had campaigned against abortion—the procedure had been largely illegal. The Court had placed limits on abortion, but now any woman or teenage girl whose pregnancy had not progressed past the second trimester could walk into an abortion clinic in any state in America and terminate her pregnancy. According to the Alan Guttmacher Institute, a New York–based foundation that studies reproductive health issues and advocates abortion rights, in 1969—the final year before states started liberalizing their abortion laws—there were virtually no legal abortions performed in the United States. In 1972, after some degree of liberalization, there were some 600,000 abortions performed in the United States. In 1973, the year of the *Roe v. Wade* decision, that number jumped to nearly 800,000. By 1975 the number of abortions performed in the United States had reached more than a million.

A PUBLIC CLOSELY DIVIDED

One year after *Roe v. Wade,* the Gallup Organization reported that the American public was closely divided on the issue of abortion. Gallup's polling had, between 1969 and 1972, recorded an increase in public support for first-trimester abortions. Still, the 1974 survey revealed no broad consensus: 47 percent of respondents were in agreement with the Supreme Court decision, and 44 percent opposed. The Gallup Organization reported comments from some of its respondents that reflected the divisions on the issue:

- ✓ A 30-year-old teacher from Alexandria, Virginia, said, "I feel it is up to the individual and not to government to dictate what may or may not be done with one's own body. I do not feel that a fetus is an individual, but an extension of the woman's body."
- ✓ A Wisconsin housewife said, "I believe abortion is murder. I say this even though I had an abortion 10 years ago. The terrible deed will remain in my heart until I die. I can't believe other women feel no remorse afterward."
- ✓ A 61-year-old salesman from Baltimore said, "Our country is loaded with unwanted, unloved children who grow up to cause many of the country's problems. This law will aid in preventing many of these births. Also the anguish and torment involved in these cases will be curtailed to some extent."

EXCERPTS FROM THE SUPREME COURT'S *ROE V. WADE* DECISION

The Constitution does not explicitly mention any right of privacy. In a line of decisions, however . . . the Court has recognized that a right of personal privacy, or a guarantee of certain areas or zones of privacy, does exist under the Constitution. . . . These decisions make it clear that only personal rights that can be deemed "fundamental" or "implicit in the concept of ordered liberty" . . . are included in this guarantee of personal privacy. . . .

This right of privacy, whether it be founded in the Fourteenth Amendment's concept of personal liberty and restrictions upon state action, as we feel it is, or, as the District Court determined, in the Ninth Amendment's reservation of rights to the people, is broad enough to encompass a woman's decision whether or not to terminate her pregnancy. . . .

On the basis of elements such as these, appellant and some amici [legal allies] argue that the woman's right is absolute and that she is entitled to terminate her pregnancy at whatever time, in whatever way, and for whatever reason she alone chooses. With this we do not agree. . . . [A] State may properly assert important interests in safeguarding health, in maintaining medical standards, and in protecting potential life. At some point in pregnancy, these respective interests become sufficiently compelling to sustain regulation of the factors that govern the abortion decision. The privacy right involved, therefore, cannot be said to be absolute.

—Justice Harry Blackmun, writing for the majority

* * * * *

I have difficulty in concluding, as the Court does, that the right of "privacy" is involved in this case. Texas, by the statute here challenged, bars the performance of a medical abortion by a licensed physician on a plaintiff such as Roe. A transaction resulting in an operation such as this is not "private" in the ordinary usage of that word. Nor is the "privacy" that the Court finds here even a distant relative of the freedom from searches and seizures protected by the Fourth Amendment to the Constitution, which the Court has referred to as embodying a right to privacy. . . .

. . . The decision here to break pregnancy into three distinct terms and to outline the permissible restrictions the State may impose in each one, for example, partakes more of judicial legislation than it does of a determination of the intent of the drafters of the Fourteenth Amendment.

—Justice William Rehnquist, dissenting opinion

- ✓ A 19-year-old farmer from Galena, Ohio, said, "The bearing of children should be entirely optional. No family should create more children than they can give the necessary love, protection, and education to. We need quality, not quantity, in future generations."
- ✓ A 42-year-old housewife from Owensville, Missouri, said, "I am very opposed to anyone freely consenting to take the life of an unborn child. Only God has the choice of whether or not to let a baby be born. I don't think any man or woman should think they are greater than God in this matter."
- ✓ A retired federal employee from Bethesda, Maryland, said, "There actually exists in the sight of God a human from the very moment of pregnancy, and to destroy such a life is wrong, unless a real emergency exists justifying destruction. The determination of justification should never be authorized by a single doctor."

In the years following the *Roe v. Wade* decision, American women would take advantage of the country's laws permitting abortion. According to the Alan Guttmacher Institute, during much of the 1980s and early 1990s, the number of abortion procedures performed would hit 1.6 million per year. But then the rate started dropping somewhat; by 2000 about 1.3 million abortions were performed annually.

In the wake of the *Roe v. Wade* decision, abortion opponents mobilized and convinced state legislatures to pass new laws regulating the procedure. Many of those laws sought to strictly limit abortions and, after court challenges, were tossed out. Some laws survived court tests, however, as judges ruled that they conformed to the principles set down by the Supreme Court in its *Roe* decision. One of the most successful strategies employed by abortion opponents was to limit the availability of abortions to teenage girls. Forty-three states now require doctors and abortion clinics to notify parents when a teenage girl requests an abortion.

Among the most restrictive states is Pennsylvania. Under the state's Abortion Control Act, a woman who requests an abortion must receive a mandatory counseling session from a physician in which the risks of abortion are spelled out. Then the woman must wait 24 hours before the procedure can be performed. Girls under the age of 18 must have parental consent; indeed, a parent must accompany the girl to the counseling session, then return after 24 hours with the girl and sign a parental consent form.

Abortion rights advocates consider that law, as well as similar measures in other states, to be potentially harmful because, they say, teenage girls aren't likely to want to tell their parents they are pregnant. Instead, abortion rights advocates contend, girls might run away from home in search of an abortion in a less

Views on Parental Consent Laws

Do you favor or oppose a federal law requiring women under 18 to get parental consent for any abortion?

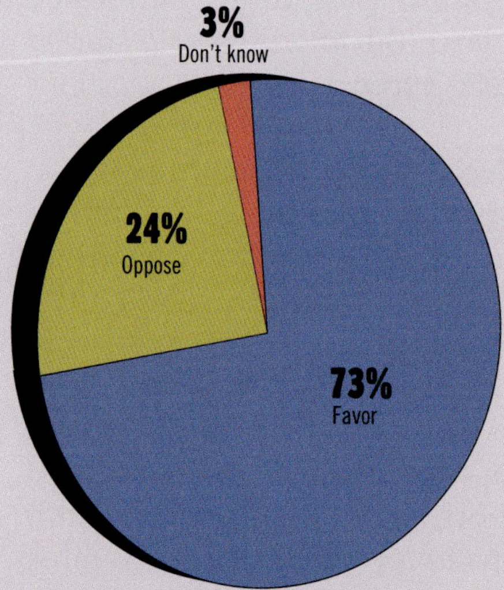

Poll taken January 2003; 1,003 total respondents
Source: The Gallup Organization

restrictive state, or they might remain silent about their pregnancy past the first trimester. Nevertheless, since 1995 no fewer than 335 anti-abortion measures have been adopted in the country's 50 state legislatures, according to the National Abortion Rights Action League (NARAL) Pro-Choice America, one of the nation's largest reproductive rights advocacy groups.

The states without parental consent laws are Connecticut, Hawaii, New Hampshire, New York, Oregon, Vermont, and Washington. In addition, the District of Columbia does not have a parental consent law.

The evidence suggests that parental consent laws have led to a decline in the number of abortions among teenage girls. In 2002 the Alan Guttmacher Institute reported that the overall abortion rate in the United States fell 11 percent between 1994 and 2000. Among adolescents, the institute said, the abortion rate declined by 39 percent.

Public opinion has long favored parental consent laws for teenage girls. In 1992 a Gallup poll reported that 70 percent of Americans favored parental consent; in 2003 the figure stood at 73 percent. Public opinion also favors a 24-hour waiting period for women seeking abortions, as well as a requirement that physicians inform women of alternatives to abortion before performing a procedure. In a 2003 Gallup poll, these measures were supported by 78 percent and 88 percent of respondents, respectively.

Parental consent, waiting period, and informed consent laws have been only one way that abortion opponents have responded to *Roe v. Wade*. They have also responded in the political arena, electing anti-abortion candidates to office. And they have responded from the pulpit, encouraging church members to become active in the campaign against abortion. But in the more than three decades since the Supreme Court's landmark decision, they have never been able to win over a majority of the American public to their position.

4 THE INFLUENCE OF RELIGION

A Roman Catholic woman recites the rosary as pro-choice protesters demonstrate at a rally. Many Christians are offended by legal abortion, arguing that it violates God's commandments.

For many Americans, opposition to abortion is rooted in religious beliefs. The Catholic Church, for example, has long opposed abortion; decades ago, women who terminated their pregnancies faced excommunication. Opposition to abortion among many conservative Protestant leaders coalesced after the Supreme Court's *Roe v. Wade* ruling. Since then, evangelical Christians have used the enormous financial power of their churches to mobilize public opinion and elect anti-abortion candidates to public office. Some religions, such as Judaism and Islam, provide their members with guidance but leave the decision on whether to terminate a pregnancy in the hands of the individual.

Over the years, the Gallup Organization has polled Americans on their religious beliefs and has consistently concluded that most Americans believe in God and regard religion as a very important factor in their lives. In 2001 a Gallup poll reported that 90 percent of the respondents believed in God, 66 percent belonged to a church, 34 percent attended church once a week, 59 percent had a "high confidence" in organized religion, and 61 percent believed that religion could address their problems.

A 2002 poll found a majority of devoutly religious Americans in support of stricter laws regulating abortion. Among respondents who attended church weekly, 65 percent said they favored stricter laws, 24 percent believed current laws were effective, and just 9 percent said abortion laws were too restrictive. "Devoutly religious Americans appear to be the most supportive of further restrictions on abortion," said a Gallup Organization analysis of the poll. "Almost two-thirds of Americans who attend their church or other place of worship on a weekly basis say they would like the nation's laws to be made more strict."

For practicing Catholics, their church's position has not changed since 1869, when Pope Pius IX declared that life begins at conception. Before Pius's declaration, there had for centuries been great debate in the Catholic Church over the moment of "ensoulment"—the time at which the fetus acquires a soul. Some Catholic thinkers and leaders held that ensoulment occurs at the time of quickening, and that the fetus is in an "unanimated" state before then. But Pius removed the distinction between the "unanimated" and the "animated" fetus, decreeing any willful abortion morally unacceptable. Women who purposely terminated their pregnancies faced excommunication. In 1917 the Code of Canon Law written under Pope Benedict XV further defined the unborn fetus as a human child, providing rules under which babies could be baptized in the womb if there was a fear the child would be stillborn.

EQUATED TO THE HOLOCAUST

Subsequent popes have been steadfast in their opposition to abortion. The highly influential John Paul II, pope from 1978 until 2005, left little doubt about where he stood on the issue. John Paul authored numerous communications to Catholics condemning abortion. In early 2005 the pope's book *Memory and Identity* likened abortion to the Holocaust—the murders of some 6 million Jews by Adolf Hitler and the Nazi regime in the 1930s and 1940s. John Paul wrote:

> It was a legally elected parliament which allowed for the election of Hitler in Germany in the 1930s. . . .
>
> We have to question the legal regulations that have been decided in the parliaments of present day democracies.

> The most direct association which comes to mind is the abortion laws. . . .
>
> Parliaments which create and promulgate such laws must be aware that they are transgressing their powers and remain in open conflict with the law of God and the law of nature.

But not all Catholics agree. Indeed, according to Gallup polls, a significant minority of American Catholics—39 percent in 2002—do not believe abortion is morally wrong. Among Catholics in Canada, the 2002 Gallup poll found 51 percent holding that view. Thus, Catholics who support abortion rights are actually members of the majority in Canada.

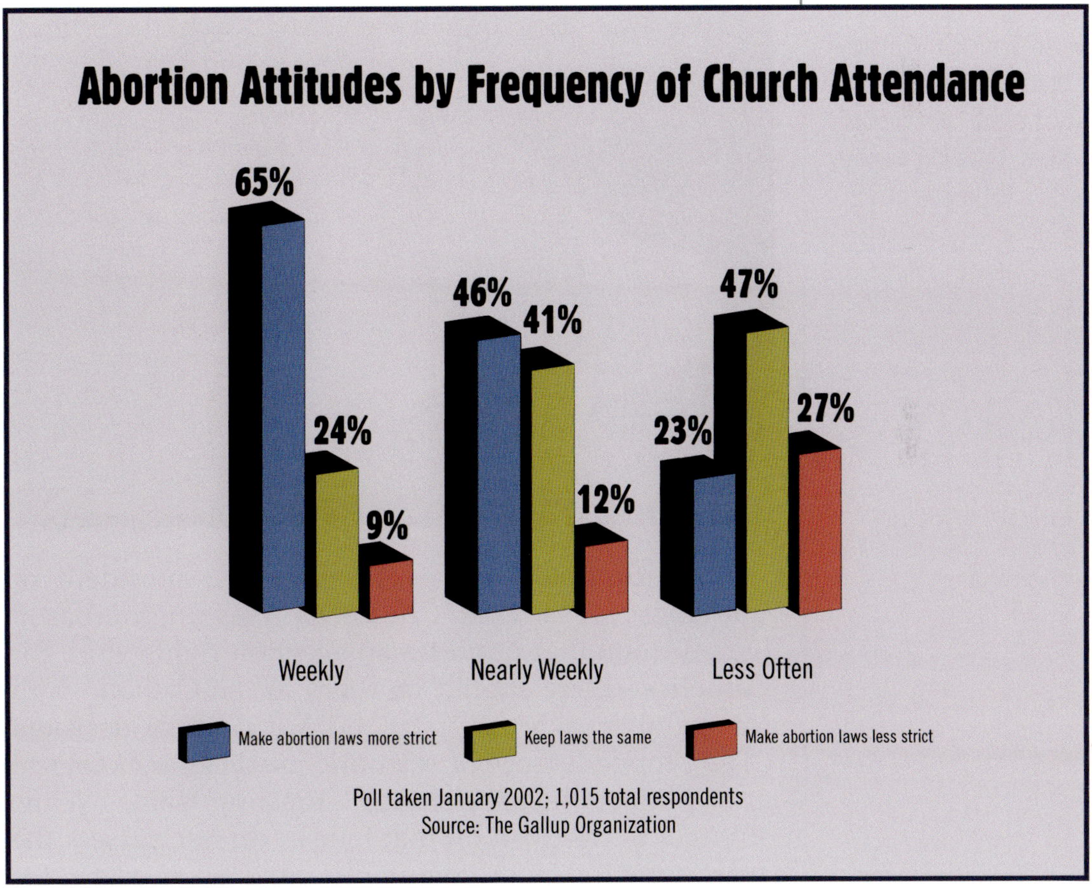

Pope John Paul II sustained the long-standing Roman Catholic opposition to abortion. In his 1995 encyclical *Evangelium Vitae* ("The Gospel of Life"), the pope wrote, "[D]irect abortion—that is, abortion willed as an end or as a means—always constitutes a grave moral disorder, since it is the deliberate killing of an innocent human being. . . . No circumstance, no purpose, no law whatsoever can ever make licit an act which is intrinsically illicit, since it is contrary to the Law of God."

According to Frances Kissling, the president of Catholics for a Free Choice—a Washington-based organization that provides an abortion rights voice for Catholics—there should be room in the Catholic faith for members who support the *Roe v. Wade* decision. "The preponderance of scientific, medical, sociological and philosophical writing," Kissling said, "leans strongly to the position that fetuses do not possess the characteristics most commonly cited as markers for personhood. Women, however, are clearly persons with the right to be treated as moral decision-makers." In addition, Kissling said, the "absolute prohibition on abortion by the church is not infallible. Therefore we defend the right of Catholics to take positions on the morality and the legality of abortion that differ from that of the church."

DISTRUST OF CATHOLICS

While the Catholic Church has publicly opposed abortion for more than a century, opposition to abortion was rarely voiced by American Protestant leaders before the *Roe v. Wade* ruling. Of course, abortion was until that time largely illegal in the United States, so there wasn't as much cause to preach against it from the pulpit. But, as many evangelical Christian leaders have since conceded, Protestants' silence on the issue also stemmed from their long-standing distrust of Catholics and of any pronouncements made by the Vatican. Harold O. J. Brown, a Harvard University theologian, observed that prior to *Roe v. Wade*, "a lot of Protestants reacted almost automatically—'If the Catholics are for it, we should be against it.' That proved to be a very unwise position, but it took a while to realize that. The fact that Catholics were out in front [on the abortion issue] caused many Protestants to keep a low profile."

That low profile changed after *Roe v. Wade*, as conservative Christian leaders devised a multi-pronged strategy for opposing abortion. They would preach against abortion from the pulpit. What's more, they would tap the potentially enormous financial power of their churches to publish books, produce films, sponsor TV shows, and take whatever other steps would be necessary to mobilize their members against abortion. In the years following the *Roe* decision, a variety of religiously based organizations were founded to lobby Congress and state legislatures on issues important to conservative Christians, including opposition to abortion. Among the most important of these groups—which also supported political candidates who shared their conservative ideals—were the National Right to Life Committee (founded in 1973), the Moral Majority (founded in 1979 by the Rev. Jerry Falwell), and the Christian Coalition (founded in 1989 by the Rev. Pat Robertson). Falwell and Robertson, in particular, became familiar faces in American culture. Both ministers hosted popular TV shows that were syndicated to independent television stations or broadcast on stations owned by their organizations.

CONSERVATIVE AGENDAS

In the months leading up to the 1980 election—the first presidential election in which abortion was a significant issue—Falwell's Moral Majority claimed to have a mailing list composed of some 7 million Protestant families, including 72,000 ministers. They were flooded with fund-raising appeals for the Moral Majority, which promised to use their donations in support of candidates who endorsed the organization's agenda. The Moral Majority denounced the spread of pornography, called for a curtailment of rights for homosexuals, and demanded selection of Supreme Court justices who would overturn *Roe v. Wade*. Donations flooded in; by the time Election Day arrived in 1980, the Moral Majority and other conservative Christian groups were reported to have funneled some $40 million into the campaigns of candidates they supported. Religiously based fund-raising activities in subsequent elections have been equally impressive.

One of the Christian leaders who dedicated himself to defeating abortion rights during this era was Randall Terry, founder of the anti-abortion group Operation Rescue. As a college junior in the 1970s, Terry saw the film *Whatever Happened to the Human Race?* The film, based on the writings of anti-abortion activist Francis Schaeffer, depicted an abortion procedure. "I literally sat there and sobbed," Terry recalled. "I remember praying, 'God, please use me to fight this hideous crime.' The Bible says, 'Rescue the fatherless from the hand of the wicked.' It's my Christian duty to fight abortion. I learned my duty from the Bible."

Terry became active in a number of anti-abortion organizations before founding his own group, Operation Rescue. The group did more than just publish anti-abortion literature, sponsor rallies, and otherwise use the media to promote its position. Operation Rescue's strategy was to send representatives to the doors of abortion clinics, where they would attempt to block access by clients. In 1987 the group led a much-publicized protest at the entrance of the Southern Tier Women's Services clinic in Binghamton, New York. Terry and the other activists waved photographs of aborted fetuses, harassed employees as they entered the clinic, and organized blockades of the clinic doors. Margaret R. Johnston, the clinic's director, told a newspaper reporter that Terry's tactics changed the face of abortion protest in America.

"He did change the landscape," Johnston said. "It went from the sort of mild-mannered Catholic older ladies to a very in-your-face, obnoxious, I'll-do-anything kind of tactic. And he did do anything."

According to the Gallup Organization, the views of Protestants on abortion closely mirror those of Catholics. In 2002 a Gallup poll found that 55 percent of American Protestants considered abortion morally wrong; in Canada, that figure was just 41 percent. Again, there is a significant minority of American Protestants who are willing to accept abortion rights, and in Canada, Protestants who accept abortion rights are members of a clear majority.

During the 1980s, groups like the Moral Majority raised money to support politicians who agreed with evangelical Christians' views on abortion and other issues.

Of course, not all Protestants are members of fundamentalist churches. There are dozens of Protestant denominations in America, and their clerical leaders take diverse views of abortion. For example, Unitarians, Methodists, and Presbyterians generally support abortion rights or at least advise their members to make their own decisions. On the other hand, denominations whose leaders steadfastly oppose abortion on demand include Southern Baptists, Jehovah's Witnesses, and the Church of Jesus Christ of Latter-day Saints (also known as the Mormons).

OTHERS WRESTLE WITH ABORTION

Other religions in America also wrestle with the abortion issue. In general, Jewish teaching has traditionally held that a fully human life is present only after the baby's head emerges from the womb. Still, Jewish tradition regards the fetus as worthy of respect and protection. While each case should be decided upon its own merits after careful consideration, most American Jews—followers of the more conservative Orthodox Judaism as well as followers of the more liberal Reform Judaism—regard abortion as permissible when the pregnancy might endanger the health of the mother. In other cases—for example, when the pregnancy has arisen from rape or incest, or when the fetus may have serious birth defects—opinions vary. Nevertheless, the majority of American Jews seem to support abortion rights as a matter of public policy. In a nationwide survey conducted in February 2000 and sponsored by the Center for Jewish Community Studies, 65 percent of Jewish respondents said they "strongly agreed," and 23 percent that they "somewhat agreed," with the statement "Abortion should be generally available to those who want it." Just 5 percent said they "somewhat disagreed," and 4 percent that they "strongly disagreed," with that statement.

American Muslims are divided on the issue of abortion. The Qur'an (or Koran)—the laws of Islam spoken to the prophet Muhammad in the seventh century A.D. by the angel Gabriel—do not mention abortion, but the Qur'an does condemn killing unless in self-defense or as a punishment for a horrific crime. Many Islamic scholars condemn abortion under most circumstances—usually they say it is permissible only if the mother's life is in jeopardy—while some scholars of Islamic law suggest that abortion is permissible within the first four months of pregnancy, the point at which Muslims believe the soul enters the fetus.

Hindus are taught to oppose abortion, but some religious scholars believe the procedure is acceptable to save the life of the mother. Buddhists are torn between the lessons of their faith, which compel them to do no harm but also to be compassionate to women who may find themselves with an unwanted pregnancy. Russian and Greek Orthodox leaders teach that abortion is permitted only to save the life of the mother.

Clearly, America is a land of diverse beliefs where many people who regard themselves as members of an organized religion must weigh what their clerical leaders tell them against the answers they may find in their own hearts.

Bishops: Say No
Communion 4 "Catholic"
Pro-Abortion Politicians
Like Kerry

5

HOW ABORTION INFLUENCES AMERICAN POLITICS

Abortion is an issue that figures to some degree in most presidential and congressional elections, though in the end it rarely seems to be a decisive factor. Candidates for national office are invariably obliged to state their position on abortion. Typically, they are pressed to express their support or opposition to abortion rights by the politically active groups that have been established on both sides of the issue. On the one side, political action committees, or PACs, have been formed by such groups as NARAL Pro-Choice America and EMILY's List, both of which provide campaign money to candidates committed to supporting abortion rights. On the other side, PACs have been formed by the National Right to Life Committee and other anti-abortion groups.

The fact is, though, that the people who donate money to those groups and vote for candidates strictly on the issue of abortion are in a

During the 2004 presidential election, a young woman outside St. Patrick's Cathedral in New York holds up a sign urging Catholic bishops to forbid pro-choice politicians from receiving Communion.

minority. Indeed, Gallup polls have consistently shown over the years that the large majority of Americans do not hold extreme positions on abortion and are willing to support candidates whose views on abortion do not agree with their own. In the fall of 2004, for example, a Gallup poll found that with regard to abortion, just 19 percent of "likely" voters "claim that the issue completely directs which candidates they are willing to support." In most cases, the economy, national defense, terrorism, crime, and similar issues have taken precedence over abortion—particularly in national elections.

THE REAGAN YEARS

The year 1980 marked the first time abortion emerged as a prominent issue in a presidential race. The incumbent, Democrat Jimmy Carter, was a devoutly religious Baptist from Georgia who taught Sunday school and talked openly of his devotion to God. Yet Carter supported the *Roe v. Wade* decision, so abortion opponents—even those from conservative Christian backgrounds—turned to the Republican candidate, Ronald Reagan. A former movie actor, Reagan had, as governor of California, signed into law a liberalization of the state's abortion laws that turned out to have sweeping consequences. But as a presidential candidate he professed to be staunchly opposed to abortion. Indeed, at Reagan's insistence, the Republican Party in the summer of 1980 adopted an anti-abortion plank in its platform—marking the first time in American history a political party had completely opposed abortion rights. The plank called for adoption of a "Right to Life" amendment to the U.S. Constitution outlawing abortion.

Jimmy Carter, a devout Christian who was personally opposed to abortion, nonetheless supported the *Roe v. Wade* decision. That position hurt him among Christian voters in the 1980 election.

Notwithstanding the GOP's anti-abortion plank, or the Democratic Party's oppo-

President Ronald Reagan poses for a photo with the justices of the Supreme Court. To the president's left is Sandra Day O'Connor, a Reagan appointee. To her left is William Rehnquist, whom Reagan elevated to chief justice. For activists on both sides of the abortion issue, the kind of justices a candidate might appoint has become a significant consideration in presidential voting decisions.

sition to it, Gallup polling in 1980 continued to show that most Americans neither supported making abortion illegal in all cases nor supported legalizing it in all cases. Rather, the majority wanted abortion legal only under certain circumstances. The 1980 Gallup survey, conducted in July, found 25 percent of respondents in favor of making abortion legal under all circumstances. That was slightly higher than the percentage favoring legalized abortion under all circumstances in 1975 (21 percent). Meanwhile, the percentage opposing abortion under all circumstances declined slightly between 1975 and 1980, from 22 percent to 18 percent. Support for keeping abortion legal only under certain circumstances remained virtually unchanged (54 percent in 1975; 53 percent in 1980). Interestingly, a Gallup analysis noted that there was not a strong correlation between party affiliation and respondents' stances on abortion. "The views of Republicans and Democrats in the current survey," pollster George Gallup Jr. wrote, "are remarkably similar."

Reagan's opposition to abortion did, however, prompt the Moral Majority, National Right to Life Committee, and similar groups to support the Republican. The religious right campaigned heavily for Reagan that year, urging evangelical Christians to cast their votes for the GOP candidate. Catholics were also urged to vote for Reagan. Shortly before the election, Cardinal Humberto Medeiros of Boston told Massachusetts Catholics that it was a sin to vote for a candidate who favored abortion rights. (As it turned out, Medeiros's position had little impact on the race. A Gallup analysis determined that Reagan won the Catholic vote by a single percentage point, which was much less than his overall margin of nine points over Carter.) By and large, though, conservative Christians did vote for Reagan in overwhelming numbers.

Still, the Republican's opposition to abortion is not believed to have been a main reason for his victory. Just 21 percent of female voters and 10 percent of male voters told the Gallup Organization that abortion represented a "bullet issue" to them, meaning that abortion was the single issue that determined their voting behavior. Rather, Reagan's victory was ensured more by widespread dissatisfaction with Carter's leadership, even among those who favored abortion rights.

As president, Ronald Reagan gave the anti-abortion movement much that it could be happy about. For starters, he appointed anti-abortion judges to the federal district courts. He also cut off federal funding for programs that provided abortions for poor people. He maintained his support for a Right to Life amendment. And when Warren Burger, Chief Justice of the United States, retired, Reagan elevated Associate Justice William H. Rehnquist to the Supreme Court's leadership position. Rehnquist was, of course, one of two justices who had issued a dissenting opinion in *Roe v. Wade.*

In 1983, a decade after *Roe v. Wade*, Reagan's popularity remained high. In December a Gallup poll reported that Reagan enjoyed an overall job approval rating of 54 percent—the president's highest rating in two years. Voters were generally satisfied with Reagan's stewardship of the economy, which was in recovery, and his get-tough stance with the Soviet Union. Again, as an issue in the national political arena, abortion seemed to be something less than a priority to most people. A 1983 Gallup poll continued to show little change in the numbers on abortion in the decade following *Roe v. Wade*—23 percent of respondents felt the procedure should be legal under any circumstances, 16 percent opposed abortion under any circumstances, and 58 percent felt abortion should be legal only under some circumstances.

By the fall of 1983, abortion rights activists knew that Reagan was riding a crest of popularity and would be difficult to beat in the presidential election the following year. But they held out hope that voters who supported abortion rights and other issues important to many women—such as the proposed Equal Rights Amendment to the U.S. Constitution—could be mobilized into an effective political bloc. Among these activists, the idea of nominating a woman who supported abortion rights to run on a national ticket began to take hold. They hoped to convince the presumptive Democratic nominee, the former vice president Walter "Fritz" Mondale, to accept a woman as his running mate.

In the summer of 1984, they turned up the heat on Mondale. By then, Mondale had the nomination sewn up. In June 1984 the National Organization for Women, which supported abortion rights as well as the Equal Rights Amendment, took out a full-page ad in the *New York Times* proclaiming, "We Want a Woman!" A few weeks later, on July 4, a group of women's rights leaders traveled to Mondale's home in Minnesota to press

Democratic presidential candidate Walter Mondale introduces his running mate, Geraldine Ferraro, who was chosen in part because of her pro-choice stance. Ultimately, the Mondale-Ferraro ticket was soundly defeated in the 1984 election.

their case. One of the women who made the trip was Betty Friedan, whose book *The Feminine Mystique* had launched the women's movement. "Fritz, you've been talking about this all your political career—equal opportunity," Friedan told Mondale. "You're one of the few who has a chance to do something about it."

The message made an impression on Mondale. A few days later, Mondale made his decision, selecting Congresswoman Geraldine Ferraro of New York as his vice presidential candidate. Clearly, Ferraro's intelligence and scrappiness would assist the ticket. As an easterner, she would help provide geographic balance to the Democratic slate. She also represented a congressional district in one of the nation's largest states, where millions of voters were registered. But most of all, Mondale hoped her commitment to abortion rights would draw women away from supporting the incumbent president.

A July 16 Gallup poll taken a few days after Mondale announced his decision revealed that female voters did respond to the congresswoman's selection. Throughout the first half of 1984, Mondale consistently trailed Reagan in the polls. The first Gallup poll taken following the Ferraro selection showed Reagan still ahead of Mondale, by a whopping 19 points, but the addition of a woman revealed a new trend in the polls. The Gallup poll found that when Reagan was pitted against Mondale one-on-one, the incumbent enjoyed a 55-36 margin. When Reagan and his vice president, George H. W. Bush, were pitted as a team against Mondale and Ferraro, the gap narrowed somewhat to 53-39. What's more, Gallup found, among women voters the Reagan-Bush ticket enjoyed only a 47-45 margin over Mondale-Ferraro, which in polling is a statistical dead heat. Said a Gallup analysis, "The gender gap is more apparent in this latest set of findings than in any test race during the last six months."

Once again, though, the issue of abortion would play a minor role in a presidential election. Americans were generally satisfied with the direction of their country. Reagan, a skilled communicator, was much beloved by a large segment of the American people, and many who disagreed with his anti-abortion policies still cast their votes for him. He won the election in a landslide. In the end, Ferraro's place on the ticket had little impact on the national race, prompting her to remark after the election, "If God were on the ticket with Fritz Mondale, even she would not have made a difference."

A MINOR ISSUE

Abortion again played only a small role in the 1988 presidential race, which matched Republican George H. W. Bush, Reagan's vice president, against Democrat Michael Dukakis, the governor of Massachusetts. Bush had formerly supported abortion rights but now was in the anti-abortion camp; Dukakis was pro–abortion rights. Early in the race, Bush and the Republicans succeeded in painting Dukakis as soft on crime—largely by virtue of an ad campaign that featured the case of a convicted murderer who had escaped from a Massachusetts prison furlough program and raped a woman in Maryland—and the Massachusetts governor never fully recovered. Crime became arguably the overriding issue in the race, and while the Gallup poll showed that the majority of Americans continued to support abortion rights under at least some circumstances, the country elected Bush, the anti–abortion rights candidate, in large measure because of his perceived tougher stance toward criminals.

A Gallup poll taken shortly before the election indicated that, once again, attitudes about abortion had changed little since *Roe v. Wade*. About one-quarter (24 percent) of the respondents favored abortion under any circumstances, more than half (57 percent) approved of the procedure only under limited circumstances, and nearly one in five (17 percent) opposed abortion under any circumstances.

WOMEN'S ISSUES

There was every reason to believe that issues important to women voters, including abortion rights, would figure prominently in the outcome of the 1992 presidential race. In 1991 Bush nominated a conservative judge, Clarence Thomas, to fill a vacancy on the Supreme Court. During his confirmation hearings before the Senate Judiciary Committee, allegations surfaced that Thomas had sexually harassed a former aide, Anita Hill. When Hill testified before the committee—which, conspicuously, had no female members—she was treated in a manner that many women found insensitive, and even offensive. But in the end, the Senate confirmed Thomas, albeit by the narrowest margin of any

Supreme Court nominee in the 20th century. Many observers predicted a major backlash at the polls the following November, particularly among female voters whose consciousness of women's issues had been raised by the Thomas confirmation fight.

Yet women's issues in general—and abortion in particular—would take a backseat in the 1992 presidential contest. Indeed, in January 1992, as the campaign was just getting under way, the Gallup poll revealed that on a list of 17 issues, abortion ranked 16th in importance among voters. Just 38 percent of respondents named abortion as an important issue for the 1992 election. In contrast, 93 percent selected the economy as an important issue—a fact that was not lost on the eventual Democratic nominee, Bill Clinton, and his staff members. Around Clinton campaign headquarters, the unofficial slogan was, "It's the economy, stupid"—a darkly

Demonstrators gather on the steps of the U.S. Capitol building to protest the nomination of Clarence Thomas to the Supreme Court. The controversy over Thomas's nomination increased awareness of women's issues.

humorous message intended to remind the candidate about the one issue most on the minds of voters. As for how the American people felt about abortion, by 1992 they still hadn't changed their minds much. Gallup reported in July that 34 percent of respondents felt it should be legal under any circumstance, 48 percent backed abortion under limited circumstances, and 15 percent believed the procedure should be illegal for any reason.

When Election Day arrived in November, the candidate favoring abortion rights, Clinton, emerged victorious at the polls. Yet as before, the election was decided by the huge bloc of voters whose views about abortion rights fell in the middle rather than at either end of the spectrum. And for enough of these voters, dissatisfaction with Bush's stewardship of the economy, which had struggled through a recession, was sufficient reason to cast their ballot for Clinton.

Clinton won reelection in 1996, but he spent much of his final term mired in scandals. The most damaging

As Vice President Al Gore watches, President Bill Clinton signs an executive order lifting abortion counseling restrictions, January 1993.

of these scandals involved an extramarital affair with a White House intern. Charges that the president had lied under oath about this relationship led the House of Representatives to vote for two articles of impeachment in December 1998. The Senate trial, held in January and February of the following year, failed to yield a conviction, and Clinton served out the rest of his term.

Given the scandals of the preceding years, it is perhaps not surprising that "family values" would be a major campaign theme of the Republican nominee, George W. Bush. For Bush—the governor of Texas and son of the former president—this included opposition to abortion. His Democratic opponent, Vice President Al Gore, was a supporter of abortion rights (though he had previously been pro-life). Again, the issue was central only to a small minority of voters in July—on average, just 17 percent of respondents to a Gallup poll reported that a candidate's position on abortion would determine their votes. Meanwhile, according to Gallup, "another 53% of likely voters said they would consider a candidate's abortion position as just one of many factors when deciding to vote, while 31% said it would not be a major issue."

In the end, Bush won the presidency in a closely contested and extremely controversial election that was decided only after the Supreme Court intervened to end legal challenges surrounding vote recounts in Florida. During his first four years as president, Bush's most significant act with regard to the abortion issue was his signing, in 2003, of legislation banning a specific procedure used in late-term abortions.

"GRAVE AND CLEAR OBLIGATION"

When Bush stood for reelection in 2004, his Democratic opponent was Senator John Kerry of Massachusetts. A Catholic, Kerry supported abortion rights—a position that prompted many members of the Catholic clergy to call for his defeat. Kerry was not alone among Catholic (and invariably Democratic) officeholders who considered the *Roe v. Wade* decision the final word on abortion rights in the United States. Even when they expressed their personal moral reservations about abortion, these politicians faced increasingly vocal criticism from their church's leaders. In 2003, for example, William Weigand, the Catholic bishop of Sacramento, California, declared that Governor Gray Davis, a Catholic, was "in very grave error" for supporting abortion rights. In South Dakota, Bishop Robert Carlson of Sioux Falls wrote to Tom Daschle, the Senate minority leader, and asked him to stop identifying himself as a Catholic because of his support for abortion rights. Another Catholic political leader, House Minority Leader Nancy Pelosi, told a reporter that she often hears criticism from church officials about her support for abortion rights. She said:

> If I was going to receive Communion, in my district in California, in my archdiocese . . . I never knew if this was the day it would be withheld. And that's a hard way to go to church. . . .
>
> In addition to that, on many occasions the archdiocese has told the nuns that I couldn't be the speaker at some event. And that's hurtful because we have so much in common. But it's the decision the church has made.

Weigand, Carlson, and the other Catholic leaders responded to the issuance of a "doctrinal note" from the Congregation for the Doctrine of the Faith, a Vatican organization charged with defending the integrity of Catholic doctrine, which declared that Catholic political leaders have a "grave and clear obligation" to oppose laws that permit abortion. The doctrinal note received the approval of Pope John Paul II before it was issued. Said the Rev. Richard McBrien, a University of Notre Dame theology professor, "You've got a Vatican that is increasingly conservative that is urging bishops who are increasingly conservative to get serious about taking on Catholic politicians who hold these views."

At their respective presidential nominating conventions in the summer of 2004, both major political parties adopted platforms that contained language about abortion. "Because we believe in the privacy and equality of women," the Democratic Party platform stated, "we stand proudly for a woman's right to choose, consistent with *Roe v. Wade*, and regardless of her ability to pay. We stand firmly against Republican efforts to undermine that right. At the same time, we support family planning and adoption incentives. Abortion should be safe, legal, and rare."

The Republican Party's platform, by contrast, asserted that "the unborn child has a fundamental individual right to life which cannot be infringed. We support a human life amendment to the Constitution. . . . We oppose using public revenues for abortion and will not fund organizations which advocate it. We support the appointment of judges who respect traditional family values and the sanctity of innocent human life."

While it is undeniable that the 2004 presidential campaign was conducted against the backdrop of the terrorist attacks of September 11, 2001, and the Bush administration's highly controversial war in Iraq, it would be a mistake to suggest that national security issues completely overshadowed all else. Divisive social issues played a significant role in the campaign as well. In fact, in a Gallup poll conducted shortly before the election, nearly one in five respondents (19 percent) said they would cast their vote solely on the basis of the candidates' positions on abortion. And among this group, Bush enjoyed a two-to-one advantage (13 percent versus 6 percent).

Although it didn't turn out to be the virtual dead heat that the 2000 presidential election had been, the Kerry-Bush race was very close. Bush's margin of victory in the popular vote was only about 3 percent. Many analysts suggested that a closely divided electorate would be a feature of American national politics for the foreseeable future. Thus, while Americans making voting decisions based on a single issue such as abortion might never constitute more than a minority, such voters could prove extremely important if one party consistently won most of their votes.

This consideration was on the minds of some dispirited Democrats who, following the 2004 election, wondered whether the time had come to rethink their party's unwavering support for abortion rights. Since *Roe v. Wade*, the Democratic Party had lost five of eight presidential elections. Despite the polling data that showed abortion was not regarded as a key issue by most voters, many Democratic leaders believed they had to take steps to open their party to include abortion opponents.

One Democratic leader, Virginia state legislator Phil Puckett, told a newspaper reporter:

Judie Brown, president of the American Life League, points to a sign labeled "The Deadly Dozen"—12 Catholic senators who support abortion rights. After losing the 2004 presidential election, some Democratic Party leaders decided to make an effort to embrace pro-life groups.

> We had a lot of people last November looking for someone to vote for besides George W. Bush. They didn't like the war or the economy—I'm talking about Russell County [Virginia], a solid Democratic county. Yet this time it went Republican—the first time ever. And it was because of moral issues like abortion.
>
> I saw it myself. I was in black churches, for example, and the pastors were saying: "This issue is important to us." There was concern about the moral direction of the country, but [John Kerry] didn't show he really shared those concerns.

University of Akron political science professor John C. Green, who has often studied Catholic voting trends, said, "The Democrats think of themselves as the party of tolerance, but they are widely perceived as not tolerant" on the abortion issue.

But Kenneth Baer, a Democratic Party analyst and former speechwriter for Al Gore, insisted that most voters favor abortion rights to some degree, and it would be foolish to turn the party over to abortion opponents. A few months after the 2004 presidential election, he told a reporter, "I cannot, for the life of me, understand why [abortion] is seen as the top priority coming out of the election. This isn't even one of the top 10. Choice is a fundamental core belief, and we should fight for it."

Still, as Democratic leaders head toward the 2008 election, they may find themselves struggling to include an anti–abortion rights voice in a party platform that has never had room for that position in the past.

6 THE DEBATE TURNS VIOLENT

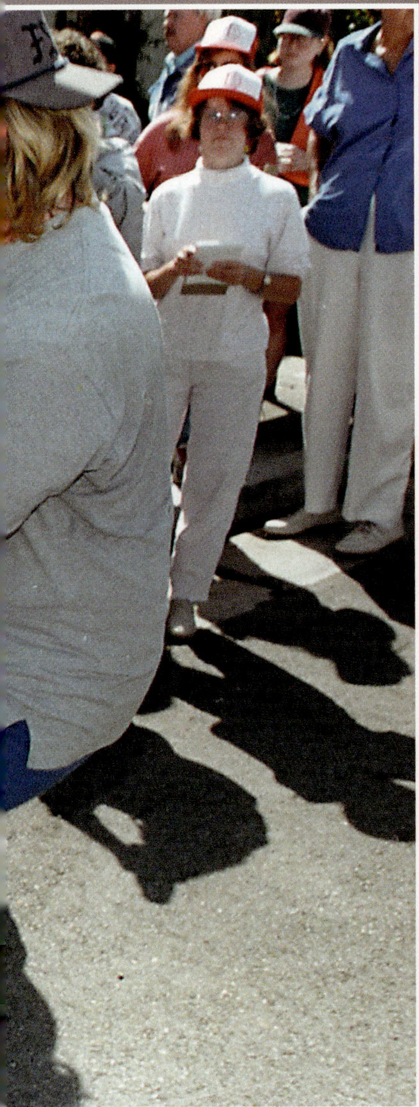

Abortion rights supporters struggle to move an Operation Rescue member attempting to block access to the Planned Parenthood clinic in San Mateo, California, July 17, 1993. On occasion, confrontations between activists on opposing sides of the abortion issue have turned violent.

By the early 1990s, abortion opponents had made real if incremental progress toward their ultimate goal of abolishing abortion on demand. The religious right had mobilized and taken up their cause. Ronald Reagan and George H. W. Bush, two presidents sympathetic to the anti-abortion movement, had instituted measures that restricted federal funding for abortions. The two presidents had also appointed many conservative judges to the federal bench, and between them had filled five vacancies on the Supreme Court (including Reagan's elevation of William Rehnquist from associate justice to chief justice). Many of these appointees, it could reasonably be assumed, might view *Roe v. Wade* with some skepticism. In 1989 the Supreme Court ruled, in the case known as *Webster v. Reproductive Health Services,* that a Missouri law prohibiting public funding for abortions was constitutional. The law also required a lung test for fetal viability after the 20th week of pregnancy—4 weeks earlier than the *Roe v. Wade* decision set as the presumed time of viability. The high court's decision gave state governments tremendous leeway in deciding how to regulate abortion.

To abortion opponents, it seemed only a matter of time before *Roe v. Wade* would be overturned. In fact, they were optimistic that the Supreme Court—led by the conservative justices appointed by Reagan and Bush—would take that step in the case known as *Planned Parenthood Federation of Southeastern Pennsylvania v. Casey.* The plaintiff in the case hoped for just the opposite outcome—that the Supreme Court would uphold *Roe v. Wade* and find

Pennsylvania's Abortion Control Act, signed into law by Governor Robert P. Casey, unconstitutional. Specifically, Planned Parenthood—a reproductive services organization—objected to provisions in the Pennsylvania statute that required women seeking abortions to receive mandatory counseling sessions spelling out the risks of the procedure, a 24-hour waiting period before an abortion could be performed, and parental consent for girls under the age of 18.

In the end, neither abortion rights supporters nor abortion rights opponents could claim a complete victory after the Supreme Court's ruling in *Planned Parenthood v. Casey*. The 5-4 decision, delivered in June 1992 and accompanied by a fair degree of acrimony among the justices, did uphold most of the provisions of Pennsylvania's abortion control law. But, in a tremendous setback for abortion opponents, it also reaffirmed the core ruling in *Roe v. Wade*—that a woman has the constitutional right to seek an abortion before the viability of the fetus.

Abortion opponents suffered another setback in November of 1992 when Bill Clinton was elected president. Once in the White House, Clinton dropped a restriction on abortions performed on military facilities, rescinded a rule prohibiting federally funded family planning clinics from providing information on abortion, and lifted the ban on the importation of RU-486, a drug that induces abortions.

INTIMIDATION AND VIOLENCE

In the wake of these developments, a small number of abortion opponents resorted to threats, intimidation, and violence in the service of what they viewed as a moral imperative: saving the lives of the unborn. But it should be emphasized that, in the long-running battle over abortion, such tactics weren't new.

Randall Terry's Operation Rescue organization had been one of the first groups to perfect tactics of intimidation. Members of the organization would target an abortion clinic and approach it in three groups. The first group, known as "rescuers," would attempt to block the doorway or the driveway of the clinic. The second group consisted of "sidewalk counselors," who would walk up to women entering the clinic and attempt to tell them of alternatives to abortion, such as placing their babies up for adoption. The third group would remain on the sidelines, providing spiritual support by singing hymns or praying.

The tactics were confrontational, and even some abortion opponents questioned whether they were advisable. In a Gallup poll taken in 1985, only 36 percent of the respondents believed that confronting pregnant

Attitudes About Restrictions on Protestors at Abortion Clinics

"As you may know, many states require protestors at abortion clinics to stay a specified distance away from the facility at which they are demonstrating. Do you think such restrictions are reasonable or unreasonable restrictions on the protestors' right to free speech?"

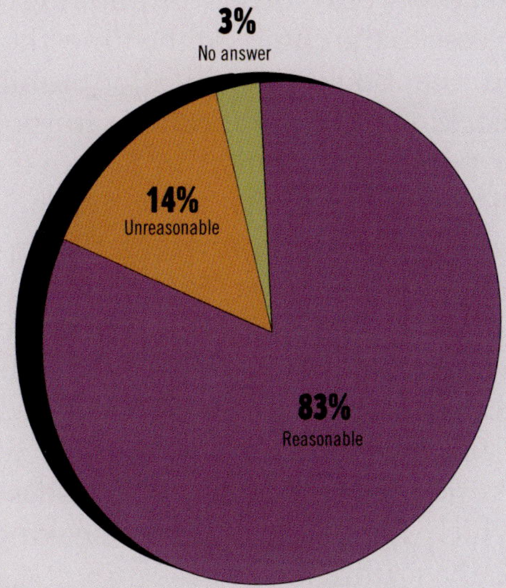

Poll taken June 2000; 1,021 total respondents
Source: The Gallup Organization

women outside abortion clinics helped the anti-abortion cause, compared with 44 percent who believed it hurt the cause. Just 8 percent of respondents said breaking into abortion clinics to destroy files or otherwise disrupt business operations helped the anti-abortion cause; 81 percent believed the tactic hurt the cause.

In 1991, during what Terry called the "Summer of Mercy," Operation Rescue targeted abortion clinics in Wichita, Kansas. "Wichita was picked for a couple of reasons," Terry recalled. "It's the heartland of America and it had an abortionist who kill[ed] babies in the third trimester. So we thought, 'Let's capitalize on the fact that there's a monster there.' And it just went wild. It just exploded. People were, like, 'Yes!' and they began coming in from all over the country. It was awesome. So we thought, 'Hey, why stay a week? Let's stay a month. Let's stay the summer. Let's see how long we can stay.'"

Operation Rescue stayed 46 days. The group's activists harassed and intimidated physicians and clients, prompting U.S. District Judge Patrick F. Kelly to issue a court order prohibiting them from blocking access to the clinic. At the time, there was no federal law on the books specifically prohibiting activists from blocking entry to abortion clinics. In the past, whenever police were called in to move demonstrators aside, they would enforce local ordinances written to control unruly crowds, not necessarily crowds in front of abortion clinics. In the Wichita case, Judge Kelly cited an 1871 law that had been written to protect freed slaves from intimidation by whites. Many Operation Rescue activists ignored the judge's order, leading to some 2,700 arrests. The court order was also opposed by President George H. W. Bush's Justice Department, which filed a legal brief seeking to overturn Judge Kelly's ruling.

While Terry's group cajoled, intimidated, and harassed, other abortion opponents tried much more dramatic—and violent—measures to shut down abor-

Anti-abortion activist Randall Terry, the founder of Operation Rescue, wears prison garb while serving time in Fulton County Correctional Institute, 1989.

tion clinics. In 1982 abortion clinics in Fairfax, Virginia, and St. Petersburg and Clearwater, Florida, were blown up by homemade bombs. Nobody was hurt in the incidents because the bombers—whose intent was to scare and send a message, not to cause injury or death—had made sure to detonate the explosives when the centers were empty. Still, the use of bombs marked a shift, by the most zealous opponents of abortion, toward more radical tactics. Regardless of their views on *Roe v. Wade*, Americans overwhelmingly disapproved of this escalation in the fight over abortion: 97 percent of the respondents in a 1989 Gallup poll believed that bombing or setting fire to abortion clinics was inappropriate, while less than 1 percent approved of such tactics.

A few abortion opponents had employed these tactics throughout the 1980s, however. Homemade bombs were exploded in clinics in Norfolk, Virginia; Dover, Delaware; College Park, Maryland; and Bellingham and Everett, Washington. On Christmas morning 1984, three abortion clinics were blown up in Pensacola, Florida, a hotbed of anti-abortion activism. Four anti-abortion activists were arrested and convicted in the bombings.

But the convictions did not end the violence in Pensacola. One of the clinics bombed in the 1984 incident was The Ladies Center. After the bombing, it was rebuilt. On March 5, 1993, a 31-year-old Pensacola factory worker named Michael Griffin spotted Dr. David Gunn sipping coffee at a local gas station. Gunn was well known to Griffin. Active in a local anti-abortion group, Griffin had participated in demonstrations outside The Ladies Center and was aware that Gunn practiced there. Years later, Griffin told an interviewer that when he saw Gunn in the parking lot, "I thought it was Providence. I knew he was getting ready to go kill children that day. I asked the Lord what he wanted me to do. And [God] told me to tell him that he had one more chance."

Memorial flowers for John Britton and James Barrett hang on a fence at The Ladies Center, an abortion clinic in Pensacola, Florida. Britton, a physician, and Barrett, his bodyguard, were killed by a former Presbyterian minister opposed to abortion.

Griffin said he walked over to Gunn's car and tapped on the window. When the physician rolled down the window, Griffin told him, "David Gunn, the Lord told me to tell you that you have one more chance." Griffin said Gunn had no response.

Later that day, Griffin stood outside The Ladies Center waiting for Gunn to leave. Griffin recalled, "I felt like I had another word from the Lord for him: that he was accused and convicted of murder and that his sentence was Genesis 9:6—'Whosoever sheds man's blood, by man his blood shall be shed.' "

Before Gunn got into his car, Griffin says, he asked the doctor, "David Gunn, are you going to kill children next week?" According to Griffin, Gunn replied by saying, "Yeah. Probably." The physician then drove away.

On March 10, Griffin waited for Gunn at a different abortion clinic in Pensacola. This time, Griffin was armed with a .38-caliber handgun. As the physician got out of his car, Griffin walked up behind Gunn and pumped three shots into his head. Griffin then dropped the gun and approached a nearby police officer, telling him, "I just shot someone, and he's laying behind the building." Gunn died two hours later. Griffin was convicted in Gunn's murder and sentenced to life in prison.

According to a Gallup poll taken shortly after the killing, 22 percent of respondents felt that Gunn's murder was "a direct consequence of the anti-abortion movement's confrontational tactics." Fifty-two percent of the respondents felt that Gunn's death could be attributed to the actions of a "fanatical individual acting on his own."

FREEDOM OF ACCESS

By the early 1990s, abortion rights supporters would estimate that some 3,000 acts of violence had been committed at women's clinics by abortion opponents. David Gunn's murder was among the most serious acts of violence, to be sure, but it would not be the last murder committed by anti-abortion activists. In 1993 Oregon mother Rachelle Shannon, who praised Griffin as "the awesomest, greatest hero of our time," traveled to an abortion clinic in Kansas where she wounded Dr. George Tiller with two shots from a handgun. Convicted of attempted murder, she was sentenced to 11 years in prison.

A year later, an abortion protester named John Salvi went on a shooting spree at two abortion clinics in Massachusetts, killing two office workers and wounding five others. He was sentenced to life in prison but committed suicide in his cell just nine months after his conviction.

The violence returned to Pensacola in 1994. On July 29, at The Ladies Center, a former Presbyterian minister named Paul Hill murdered Dr. John Britton and a bodyguard, James Barrett, with a 12-gauge shotgun. Also wounded in the attack was Barrett's wife, June. Britton had replaced Gunn as a physician at the clinic.

In an interview in prison, Hill explained that he arrived at the abortion clinic early in the morning and hid the shotgun in the grass. He described what happened when the doctor arrived with the Barretts:

> They pulled in past me, and I stepped over to where the gun was in the grass, which put the fence between me and them. Then I picked up the weapon and stepped out from behind the fence and fired three times directly at the truck. I aimed directly at the abortionist, but the driver was directly between me and him, so their heads were almost blocking one another. . . . I fired directly into him, five rounds, and then laid the shotgun down and walked away, slowly, with my hands down to my side.

Hill said he hadn't intended to kill the bodyguard, but "I realized that if I was going to have any assurance of killing the abortionist, I was probably going to have to kill him, too." As for June Barrett, Hill felt no remorse for wounding her. "She was part of the movement," he said. "She was there to protect him and to support and

"I would consider myself a martyr," Paul Hill, sentenced to death for the murders of an abortion-providing doctor and his bodyguard, said in a prison interview.

lend aid and encouragement to him. So it would certainly be justified if she had been killed. I wasn't going to turn aside from my intent to save those children from them."

A jury deliberated just 20 minutes before convicting Hill. He was sentenced to the death penalty.

The murder of David Gunn and the other acts of violence at abortion clinics prompted Congress to act. In 1994 Congress passed the "Freedom of Access to Clinic Entrances Act," which was signed into law by President Clinton. The law established jail terms and stiff fines for people blocking access by clients or doctors to abortion clinics. "We simply cannot—we must not—continue to allow the attacks, the incidents of arson, the campaigns of intimidation upon law-abiding citizens that [have] given rise to this law," Clinton said. "No person seeking medical care, no physician providing that care should have to endure harassments or threats or obstruction or intimidation or even murder from vigilantes who take the law into their own hands because they think they know what the law ought to be."

Anti-abortion activists denounced the law. Randall Terry told a reporter the new federal statute "shows the ever growing anti-Christian persecution that is coming from our government." Indeed, the federal act was only one such law written to guarantee access to abortion clinics. Several states also enacted similar statutes. In Colorado, a court challenge to that state's law would be appealed to the U.S. Supreme Court on the grounds that it violated the First Amendment right to free speech.

FIRST AMENDMENT RIGHTS

The Colorado law, passed in 1993, required protesters within 100 feet of an abortion clinic entrance to stay at least 8 feet away from people approaching the clinic unless they received permission to come closer. Three "sidewalk counselors" in Colorado—Leila Hill, Audrey Himmelmann, and Everitt W. Simpson—challenged the law, contending that it violated their constitutional right to free speech.

A Gallup poll conducted in 2000 found that the overwhelming majority of Americans disagreed with the sidewalk counselors' contention. In the view of 83 percent of the poll's respondents, Colorado had placed reasonable restrictions on abortion protesters; just 14 percent believed the statute placed an unreasonable restriction on free speech.

On June 28, 2000, the Supreme Court weighed in on the matter, delivering its opinion in the case of *Hill v. Colorado*. In a 6-3 decision, the Court upheld the Colorado statute. Writing for the majority, Justice John Paul Stevens declared that the law did not violate the First Amendment right to free speech, but merely placed reasonable restrictions on where some speech could occur in order to further an important government interest. "[T]he State's police powers," Stevens wrote, "allow it to protect its citizens' health and safety, and may justify a special focus on access to health care facilities and the avoidance of potential trauma to patients associated with confrontational protests."

In the wake of the Supreme Court's decision in *Hill v. Colorado*, many anti-abortion activists adopted new tactics to draw attention to their cause. In early 2005 a "Truth Truck" sponsored by Operation Rescue drove throughout Washington, D.C., during the week of President George W. Bush's inauguration to a second term. The Truth Truck displayed graphic photos of aborted fetuses. The vehicle then headed to Jacksonville, Florida, site of the Super Bowl. In Jacksonville, Operation Rescue hoped to reach some of the tens of thousands of visitors attending the game, as well as hundreds of news reporters from all over the world assigned to cover the event. Said Troy Newman, president of Operation Rescue, "It is not fitting that America should celebrate as if the brutal deaths of 50 million innocent children had never occurred. Our Truth Trucks will be a powerful visual reminder at these heavily attended events that we cannot turn the other way while innocent children are dying."

As for Randall Terry, the firebrand leader of Operation Rescue left the group in the 1990s after a dispute with other officials of the organization. He made an unsuccessful run for Congress in 1998 and, several years later, declared bankruptcy after losing a string of lawsuits filed against him by abortion clinics and women's groups. He remains an outspoken opponent of abortion.

7

INCHES FROM BIRTH?

In 1992 Cincinnati physician W. Martin Haskell introduced a procedure that in some quarters would be heralded as a breakthrough in preventing serious injury to women during the rare cases when it is necessary to perform an abortion in the late stages of the second trimester or in the third trimester. In other quarters, however, Haskell's procedure—called dilation and extraction, or D&X—was characterized as a barbaric and inhuman method of terminating the life of a fetus in a stage of near-viability (or full viability). Opponents labeled the procedure "partial-birth abortion" and called for a federal ban on its use. On November 5, 2003, they got their wish when President George W. Bush signed the U.S. Partial-Birth Abortion Ban Act. Within weeks, however, three federal judges had issued injunctions preventing the law's enforcement on the grounds that it might well be unconstitutional. By early 2005 the legal challenges were still pending, and it appeared highly likely that the U.S. Supreme Court would eventually be called on to rule on the constitutionality of the act.

Flanked by powerful congressional Republicans (from left: Senator Orrin Hatch of Utah, Representative James Sensenbrenner of Wisconsin, and Senator Rick Santorum of Pennsylvania), President George W. Bush signs legislation banning so-called partial-birth abortions, November 2003.

According to the Alan Guttmacher Institute, of the 1.3 million abortions performed in 2000, only an estimated 2,200 were conducted through the D&X method. In fact, the institute estimated that just 31 doctors, hospitals, and clinics in the United States practiced the procedure. "Abortions performed by dilation and extraction are quite rare," the institute reported.

Still, opposition to "partial-birth abortion" has galvanized the anti-abortion movement, spawning a new round of protest marches and litigation. On the day he signed the federal law banning the procedure, President Bush said, "For years a terrible form of violence has been directed against children who are inches from birth, while the law looked the other way." According to the president, "The best case against partial-birth abortion is a simple description of what happens and to whom it happens. It involves the partial delivery of a live boy or girl, and a sudden, violent end of that life. Our nation owes its children a different and better welcome."

In the first trimester, abortion procedures employ a technique known as dilation and curettage, or D&C, in which the cervix is artificially dilated so that a suction device can withdraw the fetal tissue from the uterus. This is the procedure used to terminate pregnancies in the so-called abortion on demand cases. All D&C abortions performed in the first trimester are legal throughout the United States.

During the second trimester, abortions are legal throughout the country, but states may regulate how the procedure is performed in order to protect the health of women. In most second-trimester cases, pregnancies are terminated through a procedure known as dilation and evacuation, or D&E. In D&E, the physician artificially dilates the cervix, then reaches into the uterus and uses a sharp surgical instrument to dismember the fetus. The final stage of the abortion requires the doctor to use a forceps to crush the skull of the fetus, so that it can be withdrawn through the cervix. This is a necessary step, because at 16 weeks the skull of the fetus is too large to fit through a partially dilated cervix.

D&X: OPPOSING VIEWS

Although D&E has been performed successfully thousands of times, it does carry risks. Since it is a surgical procedure, there is a danger that a surgical instrument might pierce the wall of the uterus, causing bleeding and possibly infection. In fact, tears to the wall of the uterus are quite common. One doctor interviewed by Salon.com reporter Margaret A. Woodbury said, "There are only two kinds of doctors who have never perforated a uterus. Those that lie and those who don't do abortions."

Another risk of D&E is that tiny parts of fetal bones may be left behind in the uterus, also potentially causing tears or infection. Still, D&E has been practiced for decades and was the common method for performing late-term abortions when Dr. Haskell developed D&X.

In D&X, the cervix is artificially dilated. Then the surgeon uses his hand to grasp the fetus and pull it, feet first, from the uterus. To get the head past the cervix, the doctor makes an incision with surgical scissors and then inserts a suction device, which collapses the skull. D&X uses fewer surgical instruments than D&E, and since the fetus is removed whole, the danger that bones or other tissue will be left behind is minimized.

Gretchen Voss, who received a late-term abortion using the D&X procedure, wrote about her experience for the *Boston Globe*. Voss said that in her 14th week of pregnancy, an ultrasound test revealed that her baby would be born with a condition known as "neural tube defect," which meant the child would be delivered with an unconnected spinal cord. If the child survived the delivery, it would face a lifetime of paralysis, brain damage, and incontinence. "Countless surgeries would be required if the baby did live," Voss wrote. "None of them would repair the damage that was already done."

Voss and her husband, Dave, made the decision to terminate the pregnancy. "Given the known as well as the unknown," she said, "we both knew what we needed to do. Though the baby might live, it was not a life that we would choose for our child, a child that we already loved. We decided to terminate the pregnancy. It was our last parental decision."

The procedure took two days. On the first day, Voss said, the physician inserted sticks of dried seaweed into her cervix.

> When I left the examining room, my mom and my husband were shocked—I was shaking and ghostly white. The pain lasted throughout the night as the sticks collected my body's fluids and expanded, dilating my cervix just like the beginning stages of labor.
>
> The next morning, Dave and my mother took me to the hospital in Boston. I was petrified. I had never had any sort of surgery, and I fought the anesthesia—clinging to the final moments of being pregnant—as I lay in that stark white room. As I started to drift off, my doctor held one of my hands, and an older, female nurse held my other, whispering in my ear, "You're going to be OK, I've been here before, lean on your husband." It was my last memory. When I woke up, it was all over.

Voss and her husband knew that their baby's severe developmental defects made its future all but hopeless. But, as she makes clear in her account, that knowledge did not make their decision to opt for a late-term abortion any less heartbreaking. Every day, Voss says, women and couples face similarly difficult situations, and she believes that if they choose to terminate a pregnancy through a D&X procedure—even during the late second trimester—that decision should be nobody else's business.

Anti-abortion activists disagree. They argue that society has a right, and a responsibility, to protect a fetus that is so close to viability (or is already viable). They also say that D&X causes intense pain to the fetus

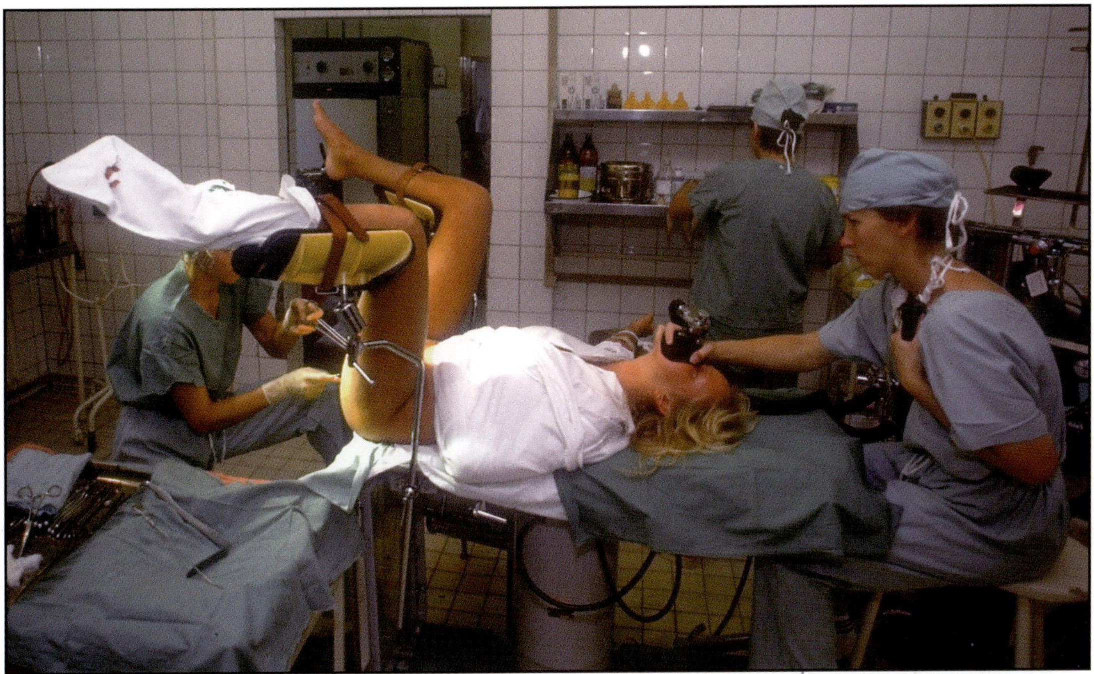

A woman undergoes an abortion in the operating room of a gynecological clinic.

and, moreover, that use of the procedure is not limited to cases, like that of Gretchen Voss, in which the child is afflicted with a serious and incurable birth defect or the mother's life is in jeopardy. Instead, opponents charge, D&X is often used simply because a woman decides late in her pregnancy that she doesn't want a child. Said Douglas Johnson, the legislative director for the National Right to Life Committee:

> Thousands of times a year, an abortionist deliberately delivers, feet first, a premature, healthy infant until only the baby's head remains lodged just inside the mother's womb. Then he punctures the base of the baby's skull with 7-inch surgical scissors and suctions out the brain.
>
> . . . The method is usually used in the fifth and sixth months (sometimes later). Babies born just after the start of the sixth month now very often survive. Even during the fifth month, if a woman goes into spontaneous labor, her baby usually will be alive when born and, therefore, legally recognized as a "live birth." Thus, this abortion method is, literally, a partial birth.

A total of 31 states passed laws banning the D&X procedure, beginning in 1995. Twenty-one of those statutes were challenged in either state or federal courts, and in all 21 cases the laws were thrown out by judges who found them unconstitutional. In one notable case, which challenged the law passed by the state legislature in Nebraska, the U.S. Supreme Court ruled in 2000 that Nebraska's statute was so vague that it criminalized all forms of abortion performed in the second trimester, including the long-accepted procedure known as D&E.

Meanwhile, in Congress the first attempt to ban D&X abortions occurred in 1995. Introduced by Congressman Charles Canady of Florida, the first version of the Partial-Birth Abortion Ban Act passed both houses of Congress but was vetoed by President Clinton. Over the next eight years the bill surfaced a

Anti-abortion protesters hold a gruesome poster outside the Supreme Court building in Washington, D.C., 1997.

number of times, but it was either vetoed again by Clinton or stalled in legislative logjams until 2003, when it finally passed both houses and was signed by President Bush. Under the law, doctors who perform D&X procedures face heavy fines and imprisonment for up to two years. The law includes an exception that permits D&X when the life of the mother is in jeopardy.

On the day the bill passed the U.S. Senate, Senator Rick Santorum, the Pennsylvania Republican who sponsored the bill, insisted that D&X is inhumane and unnecessary. "We can't allow this kind of brutality to corrupt us," Santorum said. "It makes a much more brutal and harsher country if we stand here and say, yes, for whatever reason, we are going to allow this to occur."

Responded Senator Barbara Boxer, a California Democrat and abortion rights supporter, "This is indeed a historic day, because for the first time in history Congress is banning a medical procedure that is considered medically necessary by physicians."

Soon after President Bush signed the Partial-Birth Abortion Ban Act, several federal district courts issued temporary restraining orders preventing implementation of the act until hearings could be held to determine whether it would pass constitutional muster. By the following summer, U.S. district judges in New York, California, and Nebraska had found the law unconstitutional. "Three courts in three different parts of the country have now struck down the federal abortion ban," remarked Nancy Northrup, president of the Center for Reproductive Rights, an abortion rights group. "These trial courts have been unanimous because the Supreme Court has been clear: a patient's health and safety must be a doctor's paramount concern. Congress ignored Supreme Court and medical opinion in enacting this ban. Congress claimed to be protecting women's health. In fact, they wrote a law that does exactly the opposite."

By 2005 the cases had still not been resolved, and it appeared certain that the Supreme Court would one day be called on to decide the constitutionality of the federal law banning D&X. Douglas Johnson of the National Right to Life Committee viewed the court challenges to the federal law as an opportunity for the Supreme Court to reverse its 2000 ruling in the Nebraska case. "Congress," he said, "is now inviting the Supreme Court to re-examine that extreme and inhumane decision."

Meanwhile, until the cases are resolved, some doctors have ceased practicing the D&X procedure, unsure whether the orders signed by the federal judges hold jurisdiction in all cases. Following the passage of the 2003 law, the doctor who performed Gretchen Voss's late-term abortion told her he stopped doing D&X procedures, fearful that he could face legal consequences if he continued. Wrote Voss:

> The doctor who performed my termination talks about the women he has helped through the years—the pregnant woman who was diagnosed with [cancer] and needed immediate chemotherapy, the woman who was carrying conjoined twins that had only one set of lungs and one heart, the woman whose baby had a three-chambered heart and would never live. Now, he is turning these women away. "Now, today, I can say no, but what is she going to do?" he says sadly. "What is she going to do?"

WHAT THE PUBLIC THINKS

Gallup polls have found respondents mostly opposed to late-term abortions. At the same time, the polls have found Americans supportive of abortion when the mother's life is in jeopardy or when the baby may face debilitating and painful birth defects—the two main reasons abortion rights advocates cite as justification for late-term abortions. In a 2000 Gallup poll, 84 percent of respondents agreed with the right of a woman to terminate her pregnancy when her life is in jeopardy. The same poll found less support when the impairment of the child is a likelihood: 53 percent of respondents believed abortion should be legal when the baby may be born physically or mentally impaired.

But even though abortion rights supporters insist that the health of the mother and impairment of the baby are the two main reasons for late-term abortions—an assertion, it must be reiterated, that many abortion opponents dispute—Americans are still hesitant to endorse abortion in the second trimester. The 2000 Gallup poll found 65 percent of respondents supporting abortion in the first trimester but just 24 percent endorsing the procedure in the second trimester.

In late October 2003, as the Partial-Birth Abortion Ban Act passed Congress and President Bush announced he would sign the law, a Gallup poll registered

Opinions on Late-Term Abortion, 2003

"Do you think that the procedure known as 'late term' abortion or 'partial birth' abortion should be legal or illegal?"

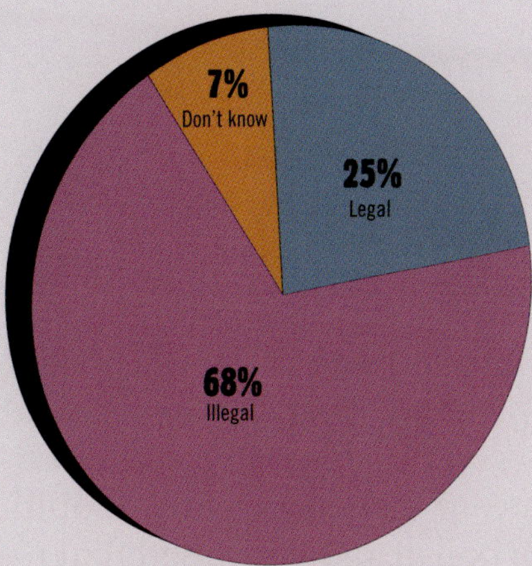

Poll taken October 2003; 1,006 total respondents
Source: The Gallup Organization

THE ABORTION PILL

In 2000 the U.S. Food and Drug Administration approved the use of a drug known as RU-486 as a nonsurgical method of abortion. Distributed in America under the name Mifeprex, the so-called abortion pill can induce miscarriages in women who are no more than seven weeks pregnant. Abortions induced by drugs are known as "medical abortions."

Use of the drug has sparked opposition from abortion opponents. Meanwhile, doctors have been hesitant to prescribe it to patients because of concerns over safety. In 2003 Holly Patterson, an 18-year-old Californian, died from endomyometritis (an inflammation of the uterus), which was allegedly caused by the drug.

The manufacturer of the drug, Danco Laboratories of New York, defended RU-486 and insisted that inflammations, infections, and bleeding occasionally follow miscarriages that are not induced by drugs. In response to a lawsuit against the company filed by Patterson's parents, Danco spokesperson Cynthia Summers told the *San Francisco Chronicle*, "No causal relationship between the use of the Mifeprex regimen and the unfortunate death of Ms. Patterson has been established. Serious and sometimes fatal infections and bleeding unfortunately occur very rarely following miscarriage and medical abortions, including following Mifeprex use, and childbirth."

Still, in late 2004 the Food and Drug Administration revised its warnings to women who take RU-486. The FDA said that while serious side effects are rare, they include infections, bleeding, and even death.

In October 2000, shortly after RU-486 was approved for distribution in the United States, a Gallup poll found Americans divided over whether the drug should be used. According to the poll, 50 percent of respondents favored the decision making the drug available, while 44 percent said they were opposed.

overwhelming public support for the measure: 68 percent of the respondents said the "late-term" abortion procedure should be outlawed, compared with just 25 percent who said that it should remain legal. However, the poll also determined that many people saw the controversy over D&X as a tactic by anti-abortion activists, including President Bush, to outlaw abortion under any circumstances. Said a Gallup analysis, "Fifty percent of Americans perceive that Bush's true desire is to ban all abortions in the United States; just over one-third disagree with this, while another 13% are uncertain. This perception is slightly higher among pro-choice Americans than it is among those calling themselves pro-life (57% vs. 46%)."

THE CONTINUING DEBATE

Whatever the intentions of President Bush and his allies in the fight over D&X, Americans remain deeply divided by the issue of abortion. Vocal (some would say extremist) minorities have staked out uncompromising positions at either end of the spectrum, keeping up a steady stream of shrill rhetoric and, frequently, demonizing the other side. Meanwhile, most Americans continue to fall

American Opinions on RU-486

"Do you personally favor or oppose the recent decision by the Federal Drug Administration to make RU-486, the abortion pill, available in the United States as a prescription drug?"

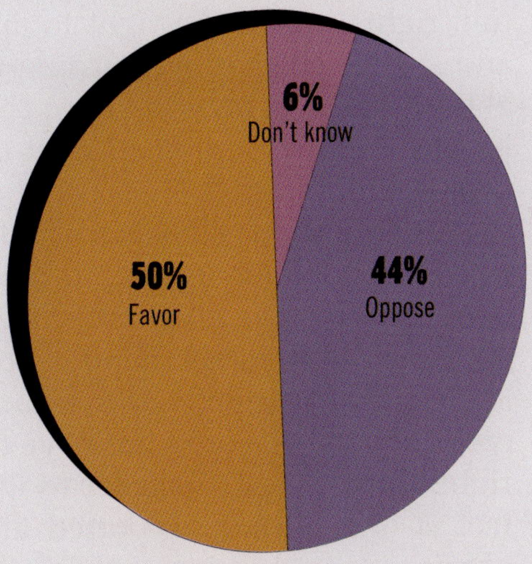

Poll taken October 2000; 1,053 total respondents
Source: The Gallup Organization

somewhere in the middle on the abortion issue, accepting a women's right to have an abortion but also recognizing certain limitations on that right.

In the fall of 2004, simmering divisions over the abortion issue once again boiled over in a political controversy. By virtue of his seniority, Senator Arlen Specter of Pennsylvania was preparing to assume chairmanship of the U.S. Senate Judiciary Committee following the November elections. An important panel, the Judiciary Committee reviews the qualifications of candidates nominated by the president for federal judgeships, including seats on the Supreme Court. As chairman, Specter would hold the power to quash nominations before they could be brought before the committee for consideration and the full Senate for confirmation.

Just before taking over as Judiciary Committee chairman, Specter made it clear that President Bush would do well to nominate candidates for the federal bench who respected abortion rights. Specter, one of the few nationally prominent Republicans to support abortion rights, called the right to an abortion "inviolate" and suggested that overturning *Roe v. Wade* would be akin to trying to reverse *Brown v. Board of Education*, the landmark 1954 Supreme Court decision that desegregated public schools.

Anti-abortion activists reacted angrily and called on Republican Senate leaders to break with tradition and deny Specter the chairmanship. For several days, it appeared that might happen, but Specter met with leaders of his caucus and assured them that federal court nominees would not have to pass a pro–abortion rights "litmus test" in order to win confirmation. "The fact is that I have supported all of President Bush's nominees in committee and on the floor," Specter told reporters. "I have never applied a litmus test."

Perhaps just to keep an eye on the moderate senator from Pennsylvania, GOP leaders in the Senate soon announced the appointment of two new members to the Judiciary Committee. Both senators—Sam Brownback of Kansas and Tom Coburn of Oklahoma—are steadfast opponents of abortion rights. Abortion rights supporters greeted the appointments of Coburn and Brownback with horror, predicting that the new members would help ensure confirmation of anti-abortion judicial nominees. Nancy Keenan, president of NARAL Pro-Choice America, said, "It appears the far right is massing troops on the border of *Roe v. Wade*."

Clearly, the conflicts over abortion will continue. In *Roe v. Wade*, the Supreme Court legalized abortion on demand, and although opponents have won some victories at the margins, abortion remains legal throughout the United States more than 30 years after the landmark 1973 ruling. Abortion is also very much a part of the fabric of American society—and regardless of whether *Roe v. Wade* is eventually overturned, it probably will continue to be. As Horatio Storer and other opponents of the procedure learned more than a century ago, even the strictest laws making abortion illegal are no guarantee that it will go away.

cervix—the neck-like part on the lower end of the uterus, through which the fetus must pass during childbirth.

dilation—widening of the cervix, which enables the fetus to enter the birth canal.

embryo—a human individual at the earliest stages of prenatal development, from the time the fertilized egg is implanted in the uterus to about the end of the eighth week after conception.

evangelical—belonging to a Protestant denomination that emphasizes the importance of personal conversion, a strict interpretation of the Gospels, and winning converts to the faith.

excommunication—the official banning of a person from membership in the Catholic Church.

fetus—a human individual at the latter stages of prenatal development, from about three months after conception to birth.

gynecology—the branch of medicine that deals with the care of women's reproductive organs.

incest—sexual relations between people who are closely related.

midwife—a female who assists women in childbirth (in the past typically without formal medical training).

miscarriage—the spontaneous expulsion of a fetus before it is viable.

obstetrics—the branch of medicine that deals with the development of pregnancy and childbirth.

placenta—a membranous organ that develops along the walls of the uterus during pregnancy and that provides for nourishment of the fetus.

pornography—material such as photographs, films, or books that depicts erotic behavior in a manner intended to cause sexual excitement.

quickening—the stage of prenatal development during which movement by the fetus is first felt.

trimester—one of the three approximately three-month-long periods of a human pregnancy.

uterus—the womb, or the place where the fetus implants itself and develops during pregnancy.

viability—the point at which a fetus becomes capable of surviving outside the womb, usually said to be at about the 24th week of pregnancy.

Blanchard, Dallas A., and Terry J. Prewitt. *Religious Violence and Abortion: The Gideon Project.* Gainesville: University of Florida Press, 1993.

Cannold, Leslie. *The Abortion Myth: Feminism, Morality, and the Hard Choices Women Make.* Middletown, Conn.: Wesleyan University Press, 2001.

Craig, Barbara Hinkson, and David M. O'Brien, *Abortion and American Politics.* Chatham, N.J.: Chatham House Publishers, 1993.

Dombrowski, Daniel A., and Robert John Deltete. *A Brief, Liberal, Catholic Defense of Abortion.* Champaign: University of Illinois Press, 2000.

Ginsburg, Faye D. *Contested Lives: The Abortion Debate in an American Community.* Los Angeles: University of California Press, 1998.

Greenhouse, Linda. *Becoming Justice Blackmun: Harry Blackmun's Supreme Court Journey.* New York: Times Books, 2005.

John Paul II. *Memory and Identity: Conversations at the Dawn of the Millennium.* New York: Rizzoli/Universe International Publications, 2005.

Martin, William. *With God on Our Side: The Rise of the Religious Right in America.* New York: Broadway Books, 1996.

McCorvey, Norma, and Andy Meisler. *I Am Roe: My Life, Roe vs. Wade, and Freedom of Choice.* New York: HarperCollins, 1994.

McCorvey, Norma, and Gary Thomas. *Won by Love: Norma McCorvey, Jane Roe of Roe vs. Wade, Speaks Out for the Unborn as She Shares Her New Conviction for Life.* Nashville, Tenn.: Thomas Nelson Inc., 1998.

Reagan, Leslie J. *When Abortion Was a Crime.* Berkeley: University of California Press, 1997.

Risen, Jim, and Judy L. Thomas. *Wrath of Angels: The American Abortion War.* New York: Basic Books, 1998.

Saletan, William. *Bearing Right: How Conservatives Won the Abortion War.* Los Angeles: University of California Press, 2004.

Terry, Randall. *Why Does a Nice Guy Like Me Keep Getting Thrown in Jail?* Lafayette, La.: Huntington House Publishers, 1993.

Weddington, Sarah. *A Question of Choice.* New York: Putnam Publishing Group, 1992.

Yarbrough, Tinsley. *The Constitutional Odyssey of Justice Harry A. Blackmun.* New York: Oxford University Press, 2005.

THE GALLUP ORGANIZATION

http://www.gallup.com

The website of the national polling institute includes polling data and analyses on hundreds of topics.

U.S. SUPREME COURT

http://www.supremecourtus.gov

By entering "abortion" into the search engine of the U.S. Supreme Court's Internet page, students can access dozens of briefs, decisions, and other documents relating to how the nation's highest court has dealt with the issue.

REPUBLICAN NATIONAL COMMITTEE

http://www.rnc.org

Dozens of speeches, press releases, and GOP position papers on abortion are available at the website maintained by the Republican National Committee.

DEMOCRATIC NATIONAL COMMITTEE

http://www.democrats.org

The Democratic National Committee maintains an archive of speeches, news releases, and other documents that explain the party's position in favor of abortion rights.

U.S. CENTERS FOR DISEASE CONTROL AND PREVENTION

http://www.cdc.gov

Numerous reports and studies on the health issues surrounding abortion are available on the website maintained by the federal government's chief public health agency.

ROE VS. WADE: 25 YEARS LATER

http://www.cnn.com/SPECIALS/1998/roe.wade

This companion website to the CNN special report produced on the 25th anniversary of the *Roe v. Wade* decision features interviews with Norma McCorvey; the full text of the Supreme Court's decision; a time line of the abortion controversy; and profiles of the principals who participated in the case on both sides.

MURDER ON "ABORTION ROW"

http://www.pbs.org/wgbh/pages/frontline/salvi

Companion website to the 1995 PBS *Frontline* documentary on John Salvi, who was convicted of killing two Massachusetts abortion clinic workers. The Internet site includes a lengthy interview with Salvi and an examination of the defendant's insanity defense.

ONLINE NEWSHOUR

http://www.pbs.org/newshour/bb/law/jan-june00/scotus_6-28.html

Reaction to the Supreme Court's 2000 decisions striking down a law banning partial-birth abortions and upholding a Colorado law making it a crime to obstruct access to abortion clinics. This website from the PBS program *NewsHour* also includes links to other abortion-related stories.

Publisher's Note: The websites listed in this book were active at the time of publication. The publisher is not responsible for websites that have changed their address or discontinued operation since the date of publication. The publisher reviews and updates the websites each time the book is reprinted.

NATIONAL RIGHT TO LIFE COMMITTEE
512 10th St., NW
Washington, DC 20004
(202) 626-8800
www.nrlc.org

Founded six months after the U.S. Supreme Court's *Roe v. Wade* ruling, the National Right to Life Committee has established itself as the chief anti-abortion voice in America. The committee includes some 3,000 local chapters, which lobby for anti-abortion laws and provide information on abortion issues to the public and press.

ALAN GUTTMACHER INSTITUTE
120 Wall St.
21st Floor
New York, NY 10005
(212) 248-1111
www.guttmacher.org

The institute conducts studies on trends in abortion, pregnancy, contraception, sexually transmitted diseases, and other reproductive issues.

CHRISTIAN BROADCASTING NETWORK
977 Centerville Turnpike
Virginia Beach, VA 23463
(757) 226-7000
www.cbn.com

The TV network that airs Pat Robertson's *700 Club* has featured many shows offering a conservative Christian view of the issues surrounding abortion. Abstracts of the abortion-related shows, press releases, and other information on how CBN has covered abortion are available on the network's website.

UNITED STATES CONFERENCE OF CATHOLIC BISHOPS
3211 Fourth St., NE
Washington, DC 20017
(202) 541-3000
www.usccb.org

The governing council of the Catholic faith in the United States. Visitors to the website can find many position papers and statements on abortion.

CATHOLICS FOR A FREE CHOICE
1436 U St., NW
Suite 301
Washington, DC 20009-3997
(202) 986-6093
www.catholicsforchoice.org

The organization serves as a voice for Catholics who support abortion rights.

NARAL PRO-CHOICE AMERICA
1156 15th St., NW
Suite 700
Washington, DC 20005
(202) 973-3000
www.naral.org

A major voice for abortion rights activists in America.

OPERATION RESCUE WEST
P.O. Box 601150
Sacramento, CA 95860
(800) 705-1175
www.operationrescue.org

This nonprofit, Christian-based pro-life organization advocates civil disobedience in its campaign to close abortion clinics.

NATIONAL ABORTION FEDERATION
1755 Massachusetts Ave., NW
Suite 600
Washington, DC 20036
(202) 667-5881
www.prochoice.org

The National Abortion Federation represents physicians and clinics that perform abortions in the United States. Students can download several clinical studies on abortion from the organization's website.

PLANNED PARENTHOOD FEDERATION OF AMERICA
434 West 33rd St.
New York, NY 10001
(212) 541-7800
www.plannedparenthood.org

The organization, founded by Margaret Sanger, promotes birth control throughout the United States. Planned Parenthood includes 122 chapters, including some that operate clinics where abortions are performed.

Numbers in ***bold italic*** refer to captions and graphs.

PICTURE CREDITS

Page:	
3:	Tim Sloan/AFP/Getty Images
8–9:	Alex Wong/Getty Images
10:	© OTTN Publishing
13:	© OTTN Publishing
14–15:	Rischgitz/Getty Images
17:	Library of Congress
17:	Library of Congress
18:	PhotoDisc, Inc.
21:	Library of Congress
23:	Bettmann/Corbis
26:	Express Newspapers/Getty Images
29:	© OTTN Publishing
31:	Bettmann/Corbis
33:	© OTTN Publishing
34:	Ronald Reagan Presidential Library
36:	Mark Perlstein/New York Times Co./Getty Images
37:	Library of Congress
42:	© OTTN Publishing
44–45:	Tim Sloan/AFP/Getty Images
47:	© OTTN Publishing
48:	Anwar Hussein/Getty Images
51:	Time & Life Pictures/Getty Images
54:	Spencer Platt/Getty Images
56:	Library of Congress
57:	Ronald Reagan Presidential Library
60:	Diana Walker/Time Life Pictures/Getty Images
63:	Luke Frazza/AFP/Getty Images
64:	Reuters/Corbis
68:	Mike Theiler/Getty Images
70–71:	Lou Dematteis/Reuters/Landov
73:	© OTTN Publishing
75:	Thomas S. England/Time Life Pictures/Getty Images
76:	Greg Smith/Corbis
79:	Charles W. Luzier/Reuters/Landov
82:	Joe Marquette/EPA/Landov
87:	Chris Niedenthal/Time Life Pictures/Getty Images
88:	Brad Markel/Getty Images
91:	© OTTN Publishing
93:	© OTTN Publishing

For almost three-quarters of a century, the **GALLUP POLL** has measured the attitudes and opinions of the American public about the major events and the most important political, social, and economic issues of the day. Founded in 1935 by Dr. George Gallup, the Gallup Poll was the world's first public opinion poll based on scientific sampling procedures. For most of its history, the Gallup Poll was sponsored by the nation's largest newspapers, which published two to four of Gallup's public opinion reports each week. Poll findings, which covered virtually every major news event and important issue facing the nation and the world, were reported in a variety of media. More recently, the poll has been conducted in partnership with CNN and USA Today. All of Gallup's findings, including many opinion trends dating back to the 1930s and 1940s, are accessible at www.gallup.com.

ALEC M. GALLUP is chairman of The Gallup Poll in the United States, and Chairman of The Gallup Organization Ltd. in Great Britain. He also serves as a director of The Gallup Organisation, Europe; Gallup China; and Gallup Hungary. He has been employed by Gallup since 1959 and has directed or played key roles in many of the company's most ambitious and innovative projects, including Gallup's 2002 "Survey of Nine Islamic Nations"; the "Global Cities Project"; the "Global Survey on Attitudes Towards AIDS"; the 25-nation "Health of The Planet Survey"; and the ongoing "Survey of Consumer Attitudes and Lifestyles in China." Mr. Gallup also oversees several annual "social audits," including "Black and White Relations in the United States," an investigation of attitudes and perceptions concerning the state of race relations, and "Survey of the Public's Attitudes Toward the Public Schools," which tracks attitudes on educational issues.

Mr. Gallup's educational background includes undergraduate work at Princeton University and the University of Iowa. He undertook graduate work in communications and journalism at Stanford University, and studied marketing and advertising research at New York University. His publications include *The Great American Success Story* (with George Gallup, Jr.; Dow Jones-Irwin, 1986), *Presidential Approval: A Source Book* (with George Edwards; Johns Hopkins University Press, 1990), *The Gallup Poll Cumulative Index: Public Opinion* 1935–1997 (Scholarly Resources, 1999), and *British Political Opinion 1937–2000: The Gallup Polls* (with Anthony King and Robert Wybrow; Politicos Publishing, 2001).

HAL MARCOVITZ has written more than 70 books for young readers. His other titles in the GALLUP MAJOR TRENDS AND EVENTS series include *Technology*, *Race Relations*, and *Drug and Alcohol Abuse*. He lives in Chalfont, Pennsylvania, with his wife Gail and daughters Ashley and Michelle, and enjoys writing fiction. He is the author of the satirical novel *Painting the White House*.